Krac's Firebrand:
Zion Warriors Book 2

By S. E. Smith

Acknowledgments

I would like to thank my husband Steve for believing in me and being proud enough of me to give me the courage to follow my dream. I would also like to give a special thank you to my sister and best friend Linda, who not only encouraged me to write but who also read the manuscript. Also to my other friends who believe in me: Julie, Jackie, Lisa, Sally, Elizabeth (Beth) and Narelle. The girls that keep me going!
—S. E. Smith

Science Fiction Romance
KRAC'S FIREBRAND: ZION WARRIORS BOOK 2

Synopsis

Section K Replication Alluthan Clone, or Krac as he was now called, had one focus in his life; protecting the descendants of the Freedom Five who ruled Earth's council. Rescued by members of the family from a secret facility, he pledged to do what he could to always keep them safe. Things become personal when insurgents target a special member of the Freedom Five, Gracie Jones-Jefe and her family. When Violet Jefe is kidnapped, he swears to do everything he can to bring the precocious little girl, who is the image of her mother, home safely and kill those who took her without mercy.

Captain "Skeeter" Lulu Belle Mann lives a life of freedom drifting from Spaceport to Spaceport in her short haul freighter looking for unusual treasures to add to her collection of mismatched prizes. On the Pyrus Space Station, she finds two treasures she has to have! One is the new navigation module she desperately needs and the other is a curly haired little girl with big green eyes that melts her heart. Never one to be denied what she really wants, Skeeter buys the first and steals the second.

When sources lead Krac to the *Lulu Belle*, he finds more than he expects - a woman who fires his blood almost as much as she draws it. Krac's hands and life are suddenly full to overflowing. He has to capture the woman who is driving him crazy, protect little Violet, and keep them all alive long enough to deliver one home and the other to his bed.

There is more than Violet in danger, though. Someone has targeted Skeeter and the *Lulu Belle* and they are just as deadly as Krac. Can he protect the feisty firebrand that has captured his heart or will he lose the only thing he has ever cared about to another of his kind?

Contents

Chapter 1

Only a sliver of the moon shone, casting a faint light in the early morning hours. It gave the assassins who moved in the shadows an extra advantage, not that they needed it. They were here on a mission and before the night was over a large number of people would be dead if they had their way.

That had been an argument the two men moving through the isolated encampment had earlier before deciding it was the only way to deter another attack on those they were trying to protect. While one wanted to get in and get out, the other wanted to send a clear message before he left. No one messed with the descendants of the Freedom Five and lived, no one.

The guard never saw the two menacing figures that moved in the darkness behind him. One shadow separated from the other. A moment later, the guard dropped to the floor, dead. In the blink of an eye, the shadow had disappeared again.

The focus of their mission was close, both could feel it. They were there to retrieve a member of the ruling family of Earth that had been kidnapped. Anastasia Miller was the direct descendent of Chance and Violet Miller.

Chance had been one of the original members of the Freedom Five, a rebel group that had fought against the Alluthans, an alien race that used up the resources of a world before moving on. His wife, Violet, had been the sister of Gracie Jones, the lone female of the group. Gracie had given up everything she knew in order to save Earth from the aliens who had captured her family and sent her into hiding. She had broken the computer language of the Alluthans. In the end, she sacrificed herself to save the Earth. That sacrifice earned her the title of being the Mother of Freedom back on Earth.

Gracie had used one of the Alluthan's own supply ships to travel to the Alluthan Mothership where she uploaded a virus she had programmed. The virus disabled the shields protecting the alien invaders and shut down the links to their power and communications systems around the globe.

With the shields, power and communications destroyed, the remaining rebel forces on Earth attacked with everything they had, defeating the suddenly defenseless Alluthan armies. Gracie had also programmed the Mothership to self-destruct. Everything was going according to plan until the Mothership turned toward the Earth, following Gracie as she desperately tried to return home.

Gracie realized that an impact by an object as large as the Mothership could destroy the Earth. Understanding there was no other way, she turned the supply ship in a desperate attempt to lead the Mothership away before it exploded. What she had not expected, or known until three years later, was that the explosion during the transition into hyperspace had not only destroyed the Mothership, it had thrown her over eight hundred years into the future. She was rescued by Grand Admiral Kordon Jefe's warship, the *Conqueror*, when signals from the damaged supply ship matched those of an unknown species that was attacking the outer colonies of the Confederation. Kordon had been tasked with finding the cause and eliminating it. Instead, he had found Gracie.

After the war, researchers spent centuries studying the aliens that had invaded their world. They eventually discovered the Alluthans could not naturally reproduce. Instead, they used a cloning system with organic material covering a rare metal skeletal system that flexed and grew depending on the information it was given. Implants were inserted into the brains of the young that developed. Each were linked and controlled through nanotechnology.

The Alluthans had captured humans and experimented on them as a desperate attempt to replace the organic material that made up their outer body. Additional findings suggested they were also experimenting with human tissue as a means for cloning additional Alluthans as their own DNA was corrupted. It was later learned that a few human researchers continued the experiments despite it being illegal to use the few Alluthans that had been captured and neutralized before they could terminate themselves.

Now, there was a new threat to Earth, this time from within. A small group of reformists, led by an unknown leader, was trying to take control of Earth by controlling or destroying the descendants of the Freedom Five who made up the majority of the council that governed the Earth.

What those who threatened them did not know was that the descendants had a very powerful and deadly adversary on their side. An adversary who would do anything to keep them safe. An adversary that was made from the monsters of their past.

* * *

Section K Replication Alluthan Clone, or Krac as he was now called, slipped back into the shadows. He paused for a brief second so he could connect with the electronic console that operated the doors. Laying his hand on the panel, he focused as he connected to the computer systems inside the encampment. Within seconds, he had taken control of it and located the information they needed.

"I found her," Krac murmured to his companion. "She is being held two floors down, last room on the left."

"You know you freak me out whenever you do that, don't you?" The other male replied under his breath. "I don't think I'll ever get used to it."

Krac ignored the softly spoken remark. "There are eight guards between here and there. Four on the first floor. One by the doors, two in a small room to the left and one at the other end leading to the second floor. There are four additional men on the same floor as Anastasia. One at the foot of the stairs and two standing outside the room where she is being held. There is one male in the room with her. You take out the one at the foot of the stairs. I will dispense with the two by the door. When I unlock the door to her cell, I will take out the male while you release her.

According to the information I have downloaded, we have less than eight minutes before additional forces arrive," Krac said calmly.

"Shit! We better get moving. Just don't fuck this up," Rorrak Jefe muttered harshly. "We need the female alive. She holds the vote that can change the rest of the Earth councils' minds. If she dies, the descendants of the Freedom Five will lose their majority on the council."

"She will not die," Krac responded emotionlessly. "Follow me."

* * *

Rorrak bit back a curse. He knew the huge gray bastard would do everything in his power to save Anastasia Miller. She had been the one to save Krac in the first place. Rorrak hadn't had the pleasure of meeting this particular council member yet, but he had heard stories of the 'steely bitch' that was known to cut through the long list of bureaucracy to get what she wanted done.

Rorrak knew very little about Krac's relationship with the council other than he was a deadly adversary when any of them were threatened. He had crossed paths with him on occasion over the past several years. Both of them had worked undercover to solve the disappearance of shipments of weapons, research scientists, and most recently, the systematic attacks on the Earth's council.

He knew Krac was only partially human, had been developed in a secret lab and that he owed his life to Anastasia Miller. One thing he did know for sure about the hybrid clone was that he was deadly in any situation. Right now, Rorrak was thankful for that as it would have been impossible to get the councilwoman out alive otherwise.

He paused at the top of the stairway leading down, waiting for the signal from Krac. He nodded once when Krac glanced at him. A shiver of apprehension went down his spine when he saw the two curved blades in the other man's hands.

Yes, Rorrak thought with a cynical curve to his lips. *If I have to go into a fight, I'd rather have Krac's cold, emotionless back covering mine than face the heartless bastard.*

* * *

Krac ignored Rorrak and focused on the mission. In truth, he could care less what the Zion Warrior thought or did. He would have preferred to come alone. It was only because of Anastasia's family's wish that the Zion agent accompany him that he had allowed the man on the special starship Anastasia had commissioned for him.

It didn't hurt that he was also very familiar with the Jefe family. Rorrak's older brother, Kordon, was now a lead councilman on Zion and was mated to Gracie Jones, a living member of the original Freedom Five. He had been skeptical of the claim that Gracie was *the* Gracie Jones until he abducted her during a previous mission. If being in her presences hadn't convinced him, the DNA scan he did proved she was a direct relation to Anastasia.

Krac felt the strange wave of heat that always washed through him when he thought of Gracie. He had kidnapped the unusual human female a little over three years before in an attempt to draw out the leader of the reformists. At the time, Anastasia thought that Altren Proctor might have been the one trying to assassinate other members of the council, specifically those who could claim a bloodline to the Freedom Five.

Krac knew immediately the human male was too weak to have organized the numerous attempts. The former councilman was just greedy. He had paid a handsome sum of credits to Krac to kidnap Gracie. Proctor had hoped to use Gracie to take control of Earth by returning the Mother of Freedom to the planet and claiming her as his mate. That plan failed miserably when another assassin Proctor hired killed the councilman as he, Rorrak and Kordon Jefe closed in on them.

Now, as he moved down the narrow winding staircase after Rorrak, his mind ran through all the information that he had downloaded. He frowned when he came to a file that was encrypted. He made a mental note to come back to it before focusing on the task at hand when they rounded the last section of the stairs.

The guard standing at the bottom turned and glanced over his shoulder. His eyes widened briefly when he realized those coming down the stairs were not part of the security team. His mouth opened, but no sound escaped as Rorrak's blade found its mark.

The man's eyes dropped to his chest and his hands wound around the sharp blade before he fell to the stone floor.

Krac moved smoothly down the steps and into the side room while Rorrak headed down the long, narrow corridor toward the other guard who was rising up out of the chair he had been sitting in.

* * *

"How much longer are we going to be in this hole," a scarred-faced man sitting at the table grumbled. "We were supposed to have moved out yesterday."

"The female is being difficult," the other man replied, sitting back in his seat and studying the tablet in his hand. "Move four spaces to the left, sling blade left to right," he muttered.

"Damn it," scarred-face cursed when the character on his tablet disintegrated. "That was my second most powerful beast."

"You should have seen it coming," the other man laughed hoarsely, tipping his head back and swallowing deeply from the flask he held in his other hand. "That is one hundred credits you owe me now."

"He won't be paying you," Krac said calmly as he ran his blade across the scarred-faced man's neck. He ignored the head that fell in the opposite direction of the body as it separated. "I want information and you are going to give it to me before I kill you."

The thin figure of the male surged from his seat, tossing the flask to one side as he drew a pistol from his waist. His scream of agony was cut short by Krac's fingers tightening around his throat. The arm with the pistol now lay on the floor.

Krac slowly walked forward, holding the paling male up off the ground until he had him pinned against the far wall. He made sure the male got a good look at him. He wanted the male to know that death had come for him and it was in the form of a creature more dangerous than he had ever seen before.

"Who is your leader?" Krac asked coldly.

"I…," the male gurgled as his eyes began to dim. "What… are…?"

Krac pulled the male forward before slamming him back against the wall. The sound of the man's head cracking against the uneven stone echoed loudly in the quietness of the room. The glazed eyes faded to blankness.

"Word of advice, Krac," Rorrak's dry voice sounded behind him. "If you want information, you have to leave your informant in one piece and not smash his head first."

Krac grunted in disgust as he dropped the male to the floor and turned with a glare. "Most species, especially the humans, are too fragile."

Rorrak looked at the bloody curved blade still clenched in Krac's left hand. He shook his head and chuckled. Not even a Zion warrior would be able to survive such a wound.

"Not all of us are made up of living metal," Rorrak replied dryly. "We have less than five minutes before more company arrives. I'd like to at least rescue the 'Princess' before they arrive."

Krac nodded. "Is your warship close?"

"Yes," Rorrak bit out. "But, we will still have a fight on our hands."

"You keep Anastasia Miller safe," Krac instructed as he headed toward the door leading down to the second level. "I'll take care of everything else."

Rorrak shrugged. "Fine with me. I just hope I don't have to carry her ass. You know how Earth women are."

Krac's eyebrow rose at the comment. Yes, he did know what most human women were like and preferred to avoid them as they were weepy, fragile and weak. He had only met two human females that gave him pause to think that they were not ordinary to the human female species: Gracie Jones and Anastasia Miller. Both of those human females confused him as neither behaved like those he had met while on Earth.

"Just protect her," Krac replied. "I will kill you if she gets hurt."

"Well, that changes everything," Rorrak muttered darkly under his breath as Krac palmed the door panel and disappeared down the second set of stairs. "I guess I'll just carry her ass then."

Chapter 2

"Tower, this is the *Lulu Belle* coming in to repair bay A4," Captain "Skeeter" Lulu Belle Mann announced cheerfully. "I need clearance of all incoming traffic. Oh, and you'd better put the bumpers out, boys, my thrusters are being a pain in the bunny butt right now. Frog! How are you doing on the repairs, sweetheart?"

"Two minutes, Skeeter! I need at least two more minutes!" The voice behind her frantically yelled.

Skeeter ignored the coarse curses coming over the system from the tower. She was used to them by now. She didn't know if it was protocol for all Spaceport Towers to use such language. She'd have to ask Bulldog, her adopted father, the next time she talked to him. She was still learning all the technical talk since he let her take over as Captain of the *Lulu Belle*. So far, it seemed to be the norm at all the Spaceports she had delivered to so far.

"Captain, I have the rear thrusters working," the high-pitched voice of her co-pilot responded. "And my name is Froget, not Frog! How many times do I have to tell you that?" The green, yellow and black creature growled as he jumped into the chair next to her.

Skeeter laughed in delight at the slightly exasperated tone of her new co-pilot. She had picked up the medium-sized amphibian creature on the Gallus Spaceport at the last minute. She didn't care what he said his name was, he looked just like the frogs in the picture vidcoms that Bulldog had given her as a child.

She had fallen in love with Frog's big eyes and long, sticky tongue. He could pick things off the wall from almost ten feet away! It was the coolest thing she had ever seen, well, until he got stuck that one time. He still hadn't forgiven her for that. How she was supposed to know that the antique paper she had picked up and hung from the ceiling was stickier than his tongue? She loved how it curled around like a streamer and she thought all the little black flying creatures on it were neat.

The only disappointment she had discovered about her new friend and co-pilot was that he didn't turn into a handsome prince when she had kissed him one night. Skeeter sighed heavily when she remembered her disappointment. She had been sure he would change as he had looked like all the frogs in the old books. Instead, he had shuddered and made her promise to never try to kiss him again.

"Thanks, Froget," Skeeter replied. "Tower, never mind about the bumpers. Frog got the rear thrusters working so I'll come in backwards."

"*Lulu Belle*, this is Tower One, please hold formation while traffic is cleared from the area," a warm voice replied.

"Oh dear, sorry about that," Skeeter whispered as she turned her short-range, class IV Trident freighter at the last minute so that she could back in between two larger long-range ships that were docked in the repair bays next to the one she had been given. The sound of metal on metal echoed through the small freighter briefly as it scraped the side of one of the larger ships as she tucked herself between them. "Tower, never mind about clearing the traffic. I was able to dock."

"Confirmed. Locks have been engaged, *Lulu Belle*, and the connection duct has sealed to the rear access door," the Tower replied. "Welcome to Newport Space Station. I'll warn everyone you have arrived."

"Thank you, Artamis," Skeeter replied warmly. "How is Tila doing?"

"Her hair is almost back to normal since your last visit. I like it blue, by the way, so please leave it that way. I'll warn my mate you have docked and will be stopping by to visit. Oh, and Skeeter," Artemis, the Tower controller replied with a hint of laughter in his voice. "Governor Erosa asks that you try to avoid Level 2 while you are here."

"You know it wasn't my fault that Bulldog went nuts!" Skeeter complained as she went through the procedure of shutting down the engines. "Lucas should have known better than to try to hire me to deal with illegal transport. I could have been in trouble with the Confederation if it hadn't been for daddy telling me what Lucas was up too. How is he by the way?"

"Lucas just got out of rehab," Artemis replied dryly. "They had a hard time re-growing his missing fingers. A very unusual problem considering his species."

Skeeter winced. Lucas was an Octoply. A species that had four arms, four legs and a dozen fingers on each hand. Her dad, Bulldog, had removed four of them on each hand when he found out Lucas had tried to use Skeeter for some unauthorized 'deliveries'. Granted, Lucas had offered her a lot of credits to do it, but she could have been in big trouble if the Confederation boarded her small freighter.

It would have been her first run for him and her most profitable since she took over the *Lulu Belle*. When she had shared her new contract with Bulldog, she had been surprised when he had calmly informed her that it had been cancelled at the last minute.

Skeeter later learned that her dad had paid a visit to Lucas. By the time he got done, Level 2 had been pretty much destroyed. She grimaced again when she thought of how many fingers the Octoply would've had to regrow.

Skeeter turned when Frog jumped down out of his seat with a loud curse. She blinked when he peered out of the portside window, then glared back at her again. She knew from the tight look around his mouth that he was upset about something she did – again. It was the fly paper look all over again.

Sighing heavily, she turned in her chair and crossed her arms across her generous chest. "Okay, what now?" She asked belligerently.

"You don't know?" Frog asked in disbelief. "Didn't you hear the sound of metal scraping? You know, that loud, I hit something, sound?"

Skeeter shrugged and dropped her hands to the well-worn arms of the captain's chair. "It wasn't that bad. It wasn't as loud as the last time. I'm not very good at backing up. Besides, it couldn't have been all that terrible. None of the alarms went off this time."

Froget Horntip looked at the pale human female pouting back at him. He had joined her crew at the last minute as a favor to her adoptive father. What the enormous Razor-tooth Triterian saw in the fragile creature biting her lower lip and looking for all the world like she didn't have a clue why he was so upset with her, Froget would never know. There was no way he would ever question Bulldog about his decision, though. Bulldog had a reputation of slashing, mutilating and digesting those who did.

Instead, he glanced once more at the large Confederation warship docked in the repair bay next to them. It now had a long…, Forget grimaced as his eyes moved over the mark,… a very, very long pink scrape down the side. He would have to fix it before the female decided she would. He shuddered as he remembered Bulldog's dire warning if anything happened to his precious but very stubborn daughter.

"Protect her, don't let any men near her and for Goddesses' sake, don't let her out into space. The girl doesn't have a single ounce of survival instinct in her body. She lives life to the fullest. I love her the way she is. Make sure she stays that way, Froget, or else."

"How do you…?" Froget remembered starting to say before the look in Bulldog's eyes turned them to a burning red. "Life... fullest... no men, no space, protect at all cost... got it."

"Good," Bulldog grinned, showing off row after row of sharp teeth. "The last bodyguard I sent didn't."

Froget looked at the clear, liquid-filled cylinder behind Bulldog and turned a very pale green at the lifeless floating body in the tank. With a sharp nod, Froget had hurried out of Bulldog's towering office. For once, he wished he had chosen a different profession than bodyguard for a living. He had a feeling he might not have a very long life expectancy in his new position.

Chapter 3

Krac nodded to Rorrak as he pulled the curved blade out of the body of the second man standing outside the door to the room holding Anastasia Miller. He silently counted to three as his hands tightened around the bloody blades. In the back of his mind, he had already mapped out the room and was calculating the probable location of the remaining male.

Raising his left foot, he kicked the door open and surged through before it had a chance to hit the floor. Twisting, he froze in mid-turn as a figure stepped out from the wall next to where the door once stood and held a laser pistol firmly against Rorrak's temple. The cold fury burning in the depths of the blue eyes staring at him caused him to raise an eyebrow.

"Don't kill him. He's with me. He thinks you are going to want him to carry your ass out of here," Krac said in a calm voice.

"Like that will ever happen," Anastasia retorted with a roll of her eyes. She dropped her arm to her side. "Who the hell are you?"

Rorrak muttered a silent curse as he released a deep breath. His eyes swept over the blood staining the back of the body on the floor before he turned to glare at the female who had taken him by surprise. Brilliant blue ones stared back at him. Another curse, this one not so silent, escaped him when he felt an uncomfortable jolt in his chest. The overwhelming urge to run like hell and knowing he couldn't held him paralyzed.

"Is he slow or something?" Anastasia asked sarcastically. "I know he can speak from his muttered curse but that doesn't mean much, so can my parrot but the damn bird still picks on the cats."

"I am not slow," Rorrak growled in a low voice. "You are hurt," he snarled as his eyes roamed over her face before his eyes darkened dangerously on her torn shirt. "How bad?"

Anastasia's eyebrow rose at the huge Zion warrior's tone. "Not as bad as that asshole. Now, if we can shelve the twenty questions for later, I'd like to get out of this shithole."

"We have company," Krac replied, tilting his head to the side. "They have found the bodies upstairs."

"Damn it all to hell," Anastasia muttered. "Is there another way out of here?"

"Yes, down the far end and to the right. There is another set of stairs leading up. It should take you close to my starship. Rorrak, take Anastasia and go. I will kill the others," Krac ordered.

"How will you get back to the *Conqueror*?" Rorrak asked.

"I'll use the transport that just arrived. Don't damage my starship. I'm partial to the modifications I made to it," Krac ordered. "Now go."

* * *

Krac walked out of the room. He knew Rorrak would protect Anastasia, not that she wasn't capable of holding her own against most adversaries. The mistake the mercenary in the other room made was being alone with the human female. Krac had witnessed Anastasia in action before and had trained with her.

He wanted information before he left and he couldn't get it with Rorrak and Anastasia here. There were times when it was best that he was alone. There were things about the Alluthans that had been hidden in their DNA and the genetic information encoded in the implants that the humans had never found. There was a reason the Alluthans used a link to control those within their forces. The humans would never really know just how lucky they were to have Gracie Jones on their side.

Krac took the stairs leading to the upper floor two at a time. He burst out of the entrance, startling the four men standing near it. The curved blades in his hands found their mark as the bodies fell. His eyes swept the long corridor, stopping on one peculiar male who was giving orders. That was the male he wanted.

He turned as several males fired their laser pistols at him. His hands arched, turning the blades flat so the short energy bursts ricocheted off them. Three men fell. The two remaining men began backing up, firing continuously at him.

Krac's eyes narrowed as they backed toward the staircase leading up. He couldn't take a chance on the man he wanted escaping. With a flick of his wrist, he sent one of the blades through the air into the chest of the mercenary next to his main target. The force of the throw impaled the man into the stone wall as the tip of the blade cut deep.

He pulled a smaller knife from the sheath in his boot and threw it next. The scream of his target as it sank deep into his right thigh echoed loudly in the long, narrow passageway. Krac walked slowly to where the man half lay, half crawled up the stone stairs.

He reached over and jerked the blade out of the man, ignoring him as he fell to the floor. Using the tip of his boot, he caught the fallen laser pistol and sent it flying against the wall. He bent over the fallen human male, grabbing the man's left wrist when he tried to bring his own blade around to stab him in the throat.

Krac shook his head as he felt the bite of the blade against his cheek instead. With a soft tsk, he broke the man's wrist. He ignored the choked, agonized cry. There would be much more before he was done.

Raising his hand to his cheek, he wiped some of the seeping blood onto his fingers before wiping it along the man's temple. Soon, he would have the information he wanted. He focused, watching in satisfaction as the male paled. Within seconds, there was no evidence of the cut that had marred his cheek just moments before.

"You have information I want," Krac said calmly. "Information that you will tell me."

"Go to hell," the human male spit out.

Krac's eyes gleamed dangerously as he gazed at the defiant eyes glaring back at him. Satisfaction coursed through him that he alone had the ability to draw out the information that he wanted. With a swift command, the nano-bots in the blood he had spread across the human's temple reacted to his command. They seeped through the male's pores and into his blood stream. Their destination, the male's brain.

"I was born there," Krac responded as he saw sweat begin to bead on the man's brow. "What is your name?"

The man's mouth tightened before his eyes glazed with pain. "Adders Weston."

"Who do you work for?" Krac asked.

"None... none... The New Order," Weston groaned, raising his good hand to his head. "Stop. Please, stop."

Krac's lips curved upward. "Tell me how you were able to kidnap Anastasia Miller."

"I...." Blood began to seep from Weston's nose as he fought against the probes searching for information. "Hinders told her about Gracie Jones. He promised to take her to meet her."

"Who is Hinders?" Krac pressed. "Is he in charge?"

"One of Miller's new bodyguards. He was here, with Miller. Dead," he choked out in a hoarse voice. "Probably dead if you are here."

"How did you know about Gracie Jones?" Krac bit out as he downloaded the flashing images rushing through Weston's brain.

"Orders came down... from the source. Don't know who. The orders come in encrypted. We were told to capture her," Weston moaned, pressing his fingers into his eyes. "Orders came down to capture Gracie Jones and return her to Earth."

Krac's mouth tightened. "Why?"

"New Order. For the New Order. To gain control. Wanted information… that Jones has. Don't know anything else. Oh God, make it stop!" Weston cried out, pulling at his hair. "Make the pain stop!"

Krac sent a silent command to the nano-bots he released into Weston. He had the images he needed, but they were disjointed. It would take days to piece the fragments together. One piece that came to him was the key to decipher the encrypted code he downloaded earlier. Perhaps there was additional information in the message.

With a single thought, he ordered the nano-bots to self-destruct in Weston's brain. The miniature explosions shredded the thick brain matter in seconds. Krac pulled his small dagger from the thigh of the dead male and stood up. His brain quickly inserted the key into the message and translated it.

A cold rage built inside as the order formed in his mind. It was time to pay Kordon Jefe a visit. Gracie was in danger once again.

Chapter 4

"What in the hell happened to the side of your warship?" Krac asked as he walked into the conference room off the bridge. "And where is Anastasia Miller?" He added when he noticed the absence of the human female.

Grand Admiral Bran Markus grimaced as muffled chuckles echoed around the room. Cooraan, the *Conqueror's* Chief Engineer, Captain Leila Toolas, the Chief Medical officer, Lazarus, the new Security Officer, and Rorrak all sat around the table. Instead, his sharp gaze swept over the male who worked specifically with Anastasia Miller's elite security team in conjunction with Roarrk Jefe's team which worked for the head council on Paulus.

"She is resting," Toolas explained. "I gave her a mild sedative despite her protests. She needed rest in order to heal."

"How badly was she injured?" Krac asked with a frown.

"Superficial wounds mostly," Toolas replied lightly, looking over at Rorrak when he sat forward. "She will be fine."

"Was she raped?" Rorrak asked harshly.

Toolas stared into the dark, flashing eyes and shivered. Both this male and the one that just walked in frightened her even though she knew they would never harm her. Both males held an air of barely controlled restraint. She sat back in her chair when the huge gray male took a step closer when she didn't answer right away.

Shaking her head, she quickly gave them what information she could without violating patient-healer confidentiality. She breathed a sigh when the new male finally sat down in the chair across from her. When she was finished, she quickly stood and excused herself.

Krac watched as the older female walked out the door. He turned and looked at Rorrak first. He had begun piecing the images from Weston together and he wasn't liking what he was seeing.

"You have to stay with Anastasia Miller and protect her," Krac stated. "The plot to kill the members on the council is larger than we originally thought. They want to use her and they want Gracie Jones for some reason. They think she has information they need."

Rorrak scowled as did the other men sitting around the table. "What information?" He demanded. "Kordon needs to be informed."

"I will be heading there. The *Conqueror* needs to return to Earth with Anastasia. She has to be there for the vote next week. All of you must make sure that she is kept safe," Krac said, shooting each male at the table a look that warned them if they failed. "I will meet with your brother and Gracie. The human did not know what information the leader was wanting from her, just that she held information that would help them."

"We will head there immediately," Bran said quietly. "Cooraan, make sure we are running at full capacity. Lazarus, I want you and Rorrak to meet with Ms. Miller and find out everything you can about her abduction. I want names, positions, diagrams of the Parliament building, everything. When are you leaving for Zion?" He asked as he turned back to Krac.

"As soon as my ship is ready," Krac responded. "A crew is preparing it now. So, what happened to yours? You do know you have a long pink line down the side, don't you?"

* * *

Bran's eyes narrowed and he shot Cooraan and Lazarus a look of disgust when both men burst out laughing. He was more than aware there was a long pink line gracing his otherwise immaculate warship. He was lucky the whole damn thing wasn't pink. If he hadn't ordered Lazarus and Cooraan to intervene it would have been.

"We had to stop at Newport Spaceport for a minor repair," Bran replied. "A short-haul freighter came into the repair bay next to us."

"Backwards," Lazarus added, trying not to laugh again. "And crooked."

"With the tower saying words even I've never heard before," Cooraan said with a grin.

"Let us just say, the Captain is very well known there," Bran commented.

"Well known?!" Cooraan laughed. "The captain is infamous! I was coming back to the ship when an all call was placed through the emergency communication's system of the Spaceport that Captain Skeeter had arrived. I've never seen so much rushing around to secure things except before a battle. The only reason I wasn't too surprised is because I know what she is like."

"So, what is this infamous captain like?" Krac asked.

Rorrak growled. "A huge, dangerous pain-in-the-ass. I met her at the same time as Cooraan and Bran. She is a walking disaster area. She is Bulldog Ti'Death's daughter. The huge Razor-tooth Triterian is very, very protective of her. I only met her once and that is once more than anyone deserves," he said with a shudder.

"What did she do?" Krac asked with a frown.

"I'll tell you what she did," Bran said, pressing his lips together as he fought a laugh. "She broke his nose and almost his nuts as well as laid Cooraan and me both out."

"At the same time?" Krac asked in disbelief. "Why would you want to fight a Razor-tooth Triterian? Even I would be challenged to defeat one in a fight."

"Oh, we weren't fighting," Cooraan muttered.

"What were you doing?" Krac asked, looking back and forth between the four men.

"Dancing," Rorrak grunted out, ignoring the laughter as he thought of the clueless redhead that had brought down the house one night long ago.

* * *

"Frog, daddy will never know, I promise!" Skeeter said in a soft, reassuring voice. "Who is going to tell him? I'm not. He might want to take the *Lulu Belle* back," she fretted. "This is my third freighter. I promised him I wouldn't tear it up."

"You are dangerous, Skeeter," Froget muttered under his breath. "You weren't supposed to go out into space. I told you I would repair the damage to the *Lulu Belle*."

"I know you did, but what about the other ship? I mean, I put a scratch on it too. It was only right to fix it," she insisted. "I didn't want you to have to do all the work. I was the one who... you know."

Froget looked at the voluptuous redheaded human female walking beside him. It had been four days since she backed into the Zion Warship *Conqueror*, leaving a long scratch down its starboard side. He should have known better than to think she would actually listen to him when he said he would take care of the damage.

He had been working on repainting the outer damage to the *Lulu Belle* when another space scooter zoomed by him. He would have recognized it anywhere. Everything aboard the *Lulu Belle* was either pink, purple, yellow, orange, red... the list just went on and on. If it was not a standard color for normal space freighters, or anything else for that matter, it was on the *Lulu Belle*.

His own room was a bright lime green with huge yellow flowers and little red and black bugs that made his mouth water every time he looked at them. They looked so real he had even tried licking them off the wall. He discovered that cold metal and paint tasted like shit.

He almost had a heart-attack when Skeeter had sailed by him toward the Confederation Warship with a paint repair kit attached to the front of her space scooter. He had already contacted the Chief Engineer to apologize and wasn't in the least bit surprised when the Zion warrior named Cooraan told him to just keep Skeeter away from the ship before expressing his condolences to Froget for being her co-pilot.

Nothing made a Goliath Amphibian species feel more confident of his early demise than having a Zion warrior issue his condolences, and sound like he meant it. Froget wasn't sure if it was because of Bulldog or because of his daughter. He suspected it was the daughter as he ducked as she swung around to look at some cloth at a merchant's stand totally forgetting she was carrying part of their navigation system in her hand.

"Oh Frog," Skeeter breathed, stepping closer to look at the sheer gray material. "Isn't it beautiful? Look how it sparkles. I bet I could make a beautiful cover for over my bed with that."

"Skeeter, we need to see if they have a replacement module for the navigation. Yours isn't going to last too much longer. I'd like to replace it so we know where in the hell we are. Space is a very big place to get lost in," Froget muttered.

"I know but isn't this beautiful? I want four meters of this, please. Frog, will you take it back to the ship for me while I go see if Artemis can help me find a part for this. I want to see Tila as well. Artemis says her hair is back to its original blue."

"I really should come with you," Froget said, looking back and forth in exasperation as Skeeter carefully counted out the credits for the material. "You go straight there. I will come for you in two hours. Nowhere else, Skeeter."

"Jeez, Frog," Skeeter scowled as she glanced down over her shoulder at him. "You sound just like daddy." Her eyes narrowed in suspicion. "He didn't hire you to babysit me, did he? The last guy he hired never came back from the bathroom. Neither did the guy before that."

"The guy before….?" Froget choked out. "How many co-pilots have you had?"

"Four, five counting you," Skeeter said, smiling her thanks to the tall, red vendor. "I think daddy fired all but one."

"What happened to the one?" Froget asked with a feeling of dread.

"Oh, he joined some religious sect on Cramoore," Skeeter replied with a shudder. "I've heard they do horrible things to the men there before they can join. Such a waste, he was really cute before I found out he was only interested in me because of daddy's credits."

Froget paled and his left hand moved down to cover his family jewels. He was very popular among the females of his species. He knew exactly what they did to the males on Cramoore.

Froget gathered the material in his arms and looked back at Skeeter. A curse escaped him when he realized she was already moving further down the crowded marketplace on Level 3. He shifted the material and scurried after her. He was not about to take a chance of being sent to Cramoore. He'd carry half the damn market if he had to but he wasn't about to let Skeeter out of his sight.

No, he thought as he hopped to catch up with his ditzy captain, *I'm going to get her back to Bulldog then retire from this life and go back into the family business. At least I'll live longer and still be in one piece.*

* * *

Skeeter laughed with joy and handed the navigation module to Artemis as she ran up the steps leading into the narrow apartments that belonged to Artemis and Tila. The ghostly pale figure of a female returned her laugh and opened her arms to engulf Skeeter in a joyful hug. Skeeter leaned back to grin up at her former nanny. She fingered a strand of the long, dark blue hair before wrapping her arms back around the slender waist and holding the closest thing to a mother she had ever had.

"I missed you, Tila. Daddy misses you too. I heard him say he should have just killed Artemis when he asked for you instead of giving in," Skeeter sighed. "How have you been?"

Tila threw back her head and laughed. Bulldog Ti'Death had purchased her twenty-two years before from a slave trader to care for his new daughter. Tila had fallen in love with her tiny charge and had been grateful to escape the heavy labor of the mines that she had been sold to. Lulu Belle had been a lively little girl with a big heart and had grown into a beautiful young woman with an even bigger one.

Tila could see how the tiny little redhead had captured Bulldog's heart. She had thought he was a dragon come to save her after all the members on board the transport had been killed by raiders. Lulu Belle had been hidden away by her parents in a desperate attempt to save her from a life of horror or death.

The transport had drifted in space for several days before Bulldog's larger shuttle came upon it. Lulu Belle had crawled out from under a hidden storage area growling and snarling until she saw Bulldog. One look and she had thrown herself into his six arms and held on to him with as much strength as her tiny arms could hold. From that moment on, she had been under the protection of one of the wealthiest and most feared species in the known star systems.

"I have been well. I am glad your father did not kill my mate. It would have made me very sad," Tila replied with a twinkle in her eye. "Come, let me fix you some tea. I made some of your favorite cookies as well when Artemis told me that you had docked. What took you so long to come visit? I expected you days ago."

"Oh, I had a little accident then we were having problems with the thrusters and then the navigation module started acting up again. I didn't want to tell daddy. I was afraid he'd want me to come home again. I thought if Frog and I could fix it first, then everything would be alright. I'm hoping Artemis can help me find a new module that isn't too expensive."

"Artemis will be happy to help you if he can. Now, tell me what you have been up to. Are you still working on your art?" Tila asked as she poured a cup of hot tea for them both.

Skeeter was thankful Artemis had pulled Froget into the other room. She wanted time alone with another female. Skeeter only had a handful of female friends, well, one really and that was Tila. She knew she could discuss anything with her and right now, she was interested in the topic of males. She had never really noticed or paid attention to them until Terry, her co-pilot who suddenly decided to join the monks on Cramoore. He had been her third co-pilot and her first and only lover. It had broken her heart when he disappeared a day after she had tried to talk to her dad about her feelings for him, at least until she found out he was only interested in her daddy's wealth.

"Tila, how did you know that Artemis was the male for you?" Skeeter asked hesitantly. "I mean. How did you know he was 'the one' for you?"

"Oh little one," Tila replied with a soft smile. "You are growing up. First, I will tell you about how I knew Artemis was my mate. Second, I will tell you what you should and should not tell your father once you have found the male for you."

Chapter 5

Zion Home World:

Krac could feel the tension building between his shoulder blades. He was being stalked. He couldn't see a damn thing in the tall ferns running along each side of him, but he could sense he was not alone. His eyes shifted as he glanced around the foliage covering the large area.

The feeling of being watched... followed... had been with him the moment he had slipped over the tall wall separating the thick forest running along the back of the compound. A low curse escaped him as he froze. He turned in a slow circle. He knew he wasn't alone. He was never wrong!

He turned back around and took several more steps forward down the narrow path. He paused again when he heard the faint sound of a twig snapping behind him. Stepping into the shadows of a nearby tree, he silently sank down into the high ferns that bordered the sides of the path.

Settling into the thick ground covering, he paused – listening. Another muffled sound to his left had him rolling onto his back. His arms moved in front of him protectively as a small dark figure burst out of the ferns and tackled him.

"Gotcha!" The voice shouted in glee.

Krac suddenly found himself struggling to get a grip on the wiggling bundle of pent-up energy that had flown into his arms. His head fell backwards as tiny size three feet barely missed his chin and nose. Lying back against the soft ground, he found himself staring up at a small, rosy face that was framed by a mass of delicate, wild blond curls. Tiny arms reached out to grab him in a fierce hug.

"Uncle Krac, I captured you!" The chubby little figure crowed.

Krac held the wiggling body of Violet Jefe up above him as he lay on his back in the flattened fern bed of Kordon and Gracie Jones-Jefe's upper garden. Vivid green eyes, shining with innocence, excitement and triumph, stared down at him in delight. Her tiny face was covered in dirt with only small patches of pale skin peeking through. Leaves and small twigs were tangled in her blond curls and she was wearing….

"What are you wearing now?" Krac asked in confusion.

"I'm a princess," Violet proudly said as she put her bare, dirty feet on his chest and, still holding his hands so she wouldn't fall, stood up. "See."

"Yes, I can see," Krac said with a twist of amusement. "I did not know Princesses wore pants under their…"

"Mommy said it is a tutu," Violet replied in a huff, flopping back down on his chest and running her tiny fingers along his cheeks. "She said I was a baller… baller…mena. But I said I wanted to be a warrior princess. Daddy said I could be whatever I wanted. Did you come to see my baby brother? Mommy had him here. She didn't have time to go to the hose-it-al. Daddy had to help mommy instead and he said I could wear my pants so I wouldn't cry." She continued to run her fingers along his face, as if tracing it.

"Where is your father now?" Krac asked, trying to decide the best way to deal with getting up as Violet looked like she was quite content to sit on his chest and run her fingers along his face. "And how did you know I was here?"

"Daddy told mommy he wasn't going to let you sneak in no more," Violet said with a frown before she leaned down and touched under his eye. "He put up a wall of pretty pictures so he could see. Do you want to see grandpa? He is supposed to be watching me while mommy and daddy and my baby brother take a nap. He smells funny and cries a lot."

"What do you mean supposed to...." Krac's voice faded when he heard Bazteen's deep voice calling Violet's name with just a touch of desperation. "Are you hiding from him again?"

Violet giggled and lay down on his chest so he was forced to wrap his arms around her as she buried her face in his neck. He felt her nod her head and giggle again. She peeked up at him.

"I did just like you taught me," she whispered. "I was really quiet while he wasn't looking."

Krac groaned. He was going to be on Kordon's shit list again. It was bad enough that Kordon kept giving him the evil eye every time he even glanced at Gracie, now he was going to be blamed for corrupting his daughter.

Well, he thought with a touch of amusement, *I did show her some tricks to use when playing 'hide-and-seek'.*

It was Gracie's fault for making me join them the last time I came here.

"Violet Cora Jefe!" Bazteen called out again, closer this time. "Little one, please come out. Your parents, not to mention your *Mi'Madue*, will never let me watch you again if you don't come out!"

"He isn't saying the magic words," Violet whispered.

"What are the magic words again?" Krac asked quietly.

"All-y in come free," she responded. "Mommy says that is when you can tell where you are without getting caught."

"How about if I distract him?" Krac offered quietly. "But, you must promise to stay right here until he says the magic words."

He watched in confused amusement as Violet peeked her head up before she buried it back in his neck with a silent nod. Krac carefully rolled onto his side and laid Violet down on the soft ground next to him. A feeling of wonder washed through him as he gently released the tiny body. She was so small and fragile and so much like her mother. They were both incredibly unusual females.

He nodded when Violet stared up at him and put her tiny index finger to her lips. He rose up out of the ferns and stepped back onto the path just as Bazteen turned around. A grin curved his lips at the dark glare that flashed over Bazteen's face.

"Hello, Bazteen," Krac said calmly, brushing dirt and leaves off his broad shoulders. "Is Kordon here?"

* * *

Bazteen stared disgruntledly at the huge male standing just a few feet from him. His eyes swept over the huge gray form of the assassin standing calmly in the secured upper garden of his oldest son's home. If it wasn't for the fact the bastard was on their side and had saved Gracie's life, even if he was the one who kidnapped her in the first place, he would have ordered him killed on sight. Of course, he had been about ready to kill Roarrk as well, even after his son explained Krac's position within the Earth's council and why he and Krac had decided to use Gracie as bait.

"He's downstairs," Bazteen replied as his eyes shifted just enough to sweep the area around Krac. "What do you want?"

"I promised to protect the descendants of the Freedom Five," Krac replied softly. "Gracie is not just a descendant, she was a member. I have news that concerns her safety.

Bazteen's eyes immediately went back to Krac's face. After a moment, he released a heavy sigh. Shaking his head, he crossed his arms over his chest.

"Where is she?" Bazteen asked, his lips twisting in amusement.

"Where is who? Gracie?" Krac asked with a raised eyebrow.

Bazteen shook his head. "No, Violet. I know she was with you. Where is that little princess hiding this time?"

Krac shrugged. "I am not at liberty to say. But I can tell you this, you must say the magic word before she will appear," he advised as he walked past Bazteen.

Bazteen's chuckle echoed through the garden. His eyes following the huge male who had no idea that he had been on the receiving end of Violet's artistic talents. Bazteen shrugged. Krac would find out soon enough. He turned back and sighed loudly before calling out the magic words. His face creased into a chuckle when he saw Violet's tangled blonde hair and mud covered face popped up out of the ferns.

"I think I'd better get you into the bath before your parents see you, little warrior princess," Bazteen commented as he studied Violet's dirty face.

"Can I have bubbles?" Violet asked, raising her hands up to be picked up. "And my toys?"

"You can have anything you want, my precious little princess," Bazteen promised.

Violet laid her head against Bazteen's shoulder and wrapped her tiny arms around his neck, hugging him tightly. "I love you, *Di' Dadre*," she said fiercely.

"I love you too, little one. I love you, too," Bazteen chuckled. "Now, let's see if I can do this without getting caught."

Chapter 6

Krac stepped lightly down the staircase leading to the lower levels of the home of Kordon Jefe. He had been here many times over the past three years. The last time was a little over a month before. Gracie has been expecting her second child any day which was why he had been chosen as Violet's new playmate for the game they were playing. Gracie was also the one who had called him 'Uncle Krac'. Violet had insisted on calling him that ever since. Krac had shrugged when Kordon had frowned in disapproval and decided he liked the new name if it irritated the huge Zion warrior. He was discovering what Gracie called 'a sense of humor'.

He slowed when he saw Kordon step out of a doorway at the bottom of the stairs. The dark scowl on Kordon's face turned to a barely suppressed smirk of amusement as his gaze swept Krac's lean form. Krac ignored him as he continued down the steps with a nod of acknowledgement.

"You know we do have a front door," Kordon said dryly. "You are welcome to use it."

Krac shrugged his broad shoulders. "Where is the fun in that?" He replied. "I need to talk with you."

Kordon nodded and stepped to one side of the door. "After you," he responded with a wave of his hand.

Krac stepped through the door, stopping short when he saw Gracie sitting in a chair near the window. An uneasy look crossed his face when he saw she had a small bundle wrapped in blue in her arms. He nodded to her when she looked up and smiled at him.

"Hi Krac. I see Violet found you," Gracie commented with a small laugh. "I guess she snuck away from Bazteen again."

Krac frowned before his face cleared in understanding. The 'pretty pictures' must have captured Violet in the upper gardens. He had to admit he was glad Kordon had installed the system. Now, more than ever, as the threat to Gracie and the descendants of the Freedom Five was escalating.

"I am glad you are both here," Krac stated bluntly. "Gracie is in danger."

Krac watched as Kordon's face darkened and Gracie's became absolutely still. The warmth that flooded him every time he saw her struck particularly hard when she bowed her head over the small bundle in her arms. He knew he would do everything in his power to help protect her.

"Tell me," Kordon said darkly, glancing at his mate when she looked back up at him. "Tell us."

"Thank you," Gracie replied softly, smiling at Kordon.

Krac nodded as he stepped toward the long bank of windows overlooking the lower front entrance. His eyes swept the perimeter before turning back to look into Kordon's dark blue eyes. He could see the cold anger burning deep in Kordon's eyes at the threat to his mate.

"Anastasia Miller, a member of the Earth Council and a direct descendent of Chance and Violet Miller, was kidnapped a little over a week ago. Rorrak and I rescued her from Tillus four days ago. They are aboard the *Conqueror* on their way back to Earth. It is imperative that Anastasia is there to cast her vote in the upcoming referendum if the descendants of the Freedom Five and other rebel groups are to remain an essential part of the council."

"Who kidnapped her and why?" Kordon asked briskly.

"The same group that Altren Proctor belonged to," Krac replied. "They have grown more aggressive and dangerous. They call themselves the New Order. They want to take over the council one way or another."

"But, why would they want me?" Gracie asked puzzled. "I'm not part of the council. I don't have anything to do with Earth, including their policies or their government."

Krac looked down into Gracie's vivid green eyes. He was still working out what some of the images from Weston meant. His own frustration grew from the fact that the leader of the New Order never appeared clear enough for him to make out any of his features.

"They think you have information that is vital to their winning," Krac replied.

"Information? What information? I know nothing of Earth's politics or even what it looks like! How could I have information that would help them?" She asked in exasperation.

"It will be alright," Kordon assured her. "I will post additional guards and let the High Council know that there is a threat to you. They will monitor all incoming and outgoing transmissions."

"It's not that, Kordon," Gracie said. "You already have a ton of added protection here. I don't want to live in a glass bowl. I don't want our children to grow up fearing for their lives either. That is why I chose to stay here, with you, instead of going back to Earth. I just don't know what information they think I can have that could help them. Everything I know is over eight hundred years old. Surely nothing can be of help to them from that long ago."

"I need you to tell me everything you can remember before you left Earth until you were found," Krac said. "There must be something you are missing. Something that they think you know and that they want."

Gracie looked down at the small bundle in her arms as he moved. Her eyes softened with love as a pair of dark blue eyes blinked several times before looking up at her. She lifted her hand to catch the tiny fingers that waved up at her and pressed them against her mouth.

"I'll tell you everything I can remember, but first I need to feed Adam," she said, looking back up at Krac. "I'll be back in a few minutes."

Both men turned as Gracie rose from her chair. Kordon walked over and caressed her cheek with the back of his fingers before brushing a kiss across her lips. Krac turned away, not wanting them to know he heard their whispered words of love. He rubbed his chest with a frown when he thought of what it would be like to have a female look at him the way Gracie looked at Kordon. Just as quickly, he dismissed it. It was fruitless to think of any female wanting a monster like him. He had learned that the hard way back on Earth.

Krac turned back around to study Kordon as the other male walked over to the bar and poured two glasses with a dark amber liquid. Krac nodded his thanks when Kordon held one out to him as he came back to sit in the chair Gracie has vacated.

"What else did you learn?" Kordon asked. "I want to know everything."

* * *

The five figures aboard the small starship gathered the last of their weapons. They had one focus, get Gracie Jones and get out. A large sum of credits was riding on them being able to capture the human female.

"Her mate will not take kindly to us taking her," Jit said. "She is bound to have additional security around her after the mess Hinders and Weston made with Miller."

"The Leader does not want excuses. We are to kill anyone who gets in our way. Moss will take out Jefe. The rest of you will take out the guards. I will get the female," Mace said. "Stick to the plan. Get in and get out. We have the information from the nurse. We know they will be taking their brat in for a checkup.

This will leave them more vulnerable as they will try to protect it."

"What if we can't get her?" Crane asked.

"Then we grab the kid. From what I have read about Gracie Jones, she will do anything to protect her brats," Harden said, snapping his laser pistol close and sheathing it at his waist. "Kill her mate, grab her kid and she'll be eating out of our hands."

"I don't want anything to do with a baby," Moss muttered. "They smell and make too much noise."

"Not the baby, you dumbass," Harden replied. "The little girl. Even if we don't kill her mate, he won't try anything if he knows we have her. That is what makes them weak, vulnerable."

"I don't like kids," Moss said. "They cry."

Harden rolled his eyes and gritted his teeth. The only reason he didn't kill the huge human male was because he was good at following orders and he was Mace's younger brother. Mace on the other hand was smart, fast and his second in command. When he paired the two brothers, they got the job done. He just had to remember he couldn't kill Moss for being a dumbass.

"Just remember," Harden said through gritted teeth. "If you can't get the female, grab the little girl. That is the Leader's orders."

"Okay," Moss replied with a shake of his head. "But, I still don't like little kids."

* * *

"I don't like this," Krac said as he glanced around the busy street. "Why are you taking the chance of leaving your compound? Surely the healer could have come to your home?"

"Normally she would have but there was an explosion west of the city at one of the factories. She is on call. Adam has been congested and running a slight fever. We would feel better if he was checked out," Kordon replied.

"We have extra guards and you with us, Krac. Surely, no one in their right mind would try anything with so many guards around?" Grace reflected as she looked at the six members of the elite guard surrounding them as they walked into the downtown office complex where their healer was located. "It would be suicide."

"I would feel better if you would have waited until the healer could come to you," Krac responded, looking around the large, open-air lobby.

"It's okay, Uncle Krac. You can beat up anyone!" Violet stated proudly as she slipped her small hand into his. "Just like my daddy!"

Krac looked down at the shiny blonde curls and wide green eyes and fought back a low curse. That damn heat was spreading through him again. He would need to control it. Emotions were dangerous. They left a person weak and vulnerable.

Still, he couldn't help the small tug at the corner of his mouth as he looked down at the little girl. It wasn't until he had gone to the cleansing room before he left Kordon and Gracie's home that he finally understood why they kept looking at him in amusement.

The little imp holding his hand had painted his face with dirt and he had perfect size three footprints running up his chest. She had placed two dark smudges under his eyes and drawn small round circles that looked like flowers on his cheeks.

He had shot Kordon a nasty glare when he came back into their den. The huge Zion warrior had burst into laughter at the disgruntled look on his face. It hadn't helped that Violet had seen him and gotten upset that he had 'washed' her pretty face paint off.

Now, he could feel himself standing just a touch straighter at the look of worship on the small face gazing up at him. For once, he did not feel like the monster he knew he was. He frowned as he thought of the effect just a few simple words spoken from a child could do and ultimately how dangerous it could be for him to believe in them.

"I will do everything I can to protect your family, Violet," he replied gruffly.

"I know," Violet said with a grin before she let go of his hand and skipped over to her mom.

Krac watched her for a moment before he started when he heard a voice next to him. A silent curse escaped him. This was exactly what he meant by being vulnerable. He had been so focused on Violet, he hadn't heard Kordon come up on his left side.

"She is a lot like her mother," Kordon said, watching as Gracie knelt down so Violet could touch Adam's cheek. "It is impossible to tell her no."

"It was unwise to bring them here," Krac insisted in a dark voice. "I want to check the surrounding area while you are with the healer. Make sure that your guards stay on alert."

Kordon flashed a fierce look at Krac. "I know how to protect my family."

"I'm not saying you don't," Krac replied calmly. "Something is not right. I can feel it. We are missing something."

Krac watched as Kordon's eyes narrowed briefly before he gave a short, sharp nod. He moved to the side as several of the elite guards moved forward to follow the small family into the lift. Only when the doors closed did he turn away. His gaze swept the lobby once more, pausing on each face for a fraction of a second so he could store the information in case he needed it later. Turning on his heel, he stepped out of the towering building in the center of the Zion capitol.

Streets filled with activity greeted him. Pulling the hood of his cloak up, he moved down along the wide walk before turning the corner that led between the towering building where he had left Kordon and his family and another. Something was wrong, he could feel it and he was never wrong.

* * *

An hour later, he stepped back into the medical tower. He frowned as he glanced at his comlink. He had linked it to Kordon's and told him to contact him when they were ready to leave. He had searched the entire area out to three blocks, slowly increasing his circle.

His scans did not show anything out of the ordinary. Now, as he stood in the lower lobby, he casually palmed the slim tablet that Kordon had given him to connect into the main communications control tower that monitored incoming and outgoing transports from the planet. He focused, sending microfiber connections from his wrist into the device. Once he had established a link, he quickly bypassed the security settings that were set to limit the end user from accessing other areas of the computer system.

He leaned back against the wall near the lift as information poured into his brain at a dizzying speed. His eyes lowered as the data poured into his mind. He bit back a groan as the pressure built until his head throbbed painfully. He was about to disconnect the link with an unusual signal caught his attention.

"Krac! Get your ass up here. Level 26," Kordon's voice furiously shouted out in his comlink, breaking his concentration. "We've got trouble."

Krac turned and slapped his hand over the control panel to the lift even as he disconnected from the tablet. His eyes flew upward as it rapidly descended. The passengers inside gripped the railing on the inside in a panic as it descended faster than normal.

He slowed the compartment at the last moment and sent an override for the doors to open before it stopped. The five passengers inside tumbled out as he swept past them. The moment he was inside, he sent

another command for the doors to close and the lift to
rise.

"What is the situation?" he asked calmly into the
comlink, ignoring the sounds of laser fire over it.

"The guards are down," Kordon responded. "The
nurse is working with the rebels. I'm not sure how
many there are. My senior guard was able to alert me
before he went down. We are barricaded in the
healer's office. Take a right out of the lift. Go down
the corridor and last room on the left. I'm not sure
how much longer I can hold them."

"I will be there in forty-three seconds," Krac
replied. "Do whatever you have to do to keep your
family safe."

"What the fuck do you think I'm doing?" Kordon
retorted.

Krac cursed silently when he heard Violet's scared
voice in the background telling her mommy that
daddy had 'cursed.' The muted cries of Adam could
be heard as well as Gracie frantically trying to
comfort both of her children.

His hands were already between the door of the
lift and the side as it began to open. He pushed
against the smooth metal, ignoring the sound of
crunching as the gears inside were stripped as he
shoved it out of the way. He rolled as laser fire filled
the interior. His own laser pistol was in his hand as he
came up and fired. A dark hole appeared through the
center of the male's forehead. The male jerked back in
surprise before falling forward over the counter of the
reception area.

Krac turned as another male fired from down the long corridor. He suppressed the dark rage building in him when he heard the sound of a small explosion followed by a loud scream and the terrified cries of Violet and Adam. He focused on the male who had pulled back around the corner again.

He stepped forward cautiously, waiting patiently for the male to reappear. He cursed when he saw a different male reappear holding a tall, slender female wearing a medical uniform in front of him.

Two other men appeared behind him. One held the stiff body of Gracie. Her arms were empty and silent tears of grief dampened her cheeks. The splattering of dark blood stained her hands and the front of her shirt. Krac paused when one of the men jerked Violet's head back by her curls and held his pistol against her temple.

"I wouldn't come any closer," the tall man holding Gracie said. "My friend here doesn't like kids. You come any closer and he'll kill her."

"Gracie?" Krac asked without taking his eyes off of the male holding Violet.

"They shot Kordon," she whispered. "He needs immediate medical attention. Please, let the healer help him. Please!" She begged the man holding her.

"I'm afraid that letting him live is not part of the plan, princess," Harden replied. "Let's go. The window's closing. Take the kid and kill the bitch."

"No!" Gracie cried out.

"Mommy!" Violet screamed.

Krac watched as Violet threw her head back, connecting with the nose of the large male holding her while her tiny feet kicked wildly to get free. Gracie and the healer reacted at the same time, turning on their captors. The healer brought her hand around, hitting her captor in the mouth while Gracie slammed her heel into the male holding her and jerked forward. She reached for Violet at the same time as Krac let out a shot from his pistol at the male who had been holding the healer.

A loud roar sounded from the larger male as he grabbed the wounded man around the waist and threw him over his shoulder while pulling Violet's struggling body up in his other arm. Krac ignored the stinging as multiple shots struck him in the chest, arm and leg as he continued firing at the three males. Gracie cried out as the healer wrapped her arms around her and pulled her away from the men.

"NO!" Gracie screamed, fighting to break free as the men pushed through another door. "Violet! NO!"

Krac ignored the burning from the numerous wounds on his body as he ran the rest of the way down the narrow corridor. His only thought was to get to Violet. He grabbed Gracie around her waist, turning as he did, and slammed his shoulder into the heavy metal door. He released Gracie and slammed into it again. The metal groaned under the force of the impact.

"Take care of Kordon," he growled through gritted teeth before slamming into the door again. "Now!"

The healer nodded and stumbled up and into the other room where Kordon lay motionless on the floor. Blood pooled around his body. Krac ignored all of that as the door finally gave way. He stumbled before running for the open window.

His eyes quickly scanned the area, but there was no sign of the transport the men had used to get away. His eyes lowered to the ground twenty-six floors below. Life below remained untouched by the violence happening high above them.

He turned, his hand already running through the information on scheduled departures at the same time as he sent a level five alert with information about the abduction of High Councilman Kordon Jefe's daughter and the attack on him and his family to Rorrak and other members of the council Rorrak assured him could be trusted.

"What is his condition?" Bazteen Jefe demanded immediately over the connection. "Additional guards are on their way."

"Lock down all departures," Krac responded. "I was able to kill one of the attackers. The healer is working on Kordon."

He paused inside the door of the healer's office. Gracie sat on the floor next to Kordon's head. She was gently stroking his hair and face with one hand while Adam's small body was tucked against her with the other. The healer was speaking quietly into her comlink while placing a stabilizer over the large wound to his chest.

"Krac?" Gracie whispered, looking up at him with eyes filled with a quiet grief. "Is she…? Is she…?"

"No," Krac interrupted harshly. "They took her. They will not harm her, Gracie. They wanted you. They will use her to get to you. They cannot do that if they harm her. Will he live?" He asked the healer.

"Yes," the healer replied with determination. "I will not lose him. I have an emergency team that should be here any moment."

The sound of running feet echoed before her words finished leaving her lips. Krac turned immediately and scanned those coming in. He stood to the side as Kordon was lifted onto a stretcher and a portable life support was attached to him. One of the medics who came in bent and carefully helped Gracie up.

"Krac, find her for us," Gracie whispered as she watched their healer nod for the group to move toward the lift. "Please… please find her and bring her ho… home."

"I will find her, Gracie," Krac promised. "I will find her and I will kill every one of those responsible for this."

"I can't… I can't lose them," Gracie choked out, holding Adam closer against her. "I can't. Not after losing everything else. Even Murphy can't be that cruel."

"Murphy?" Krac asked, puzzled.

"Murphy's Law," Gracie mumbled. "I have to go with him. I love him so much. Find Violet, Krac. I'm trusting you. You are the only one right now that I can trust to find her and bring her home safely."

Krac watched as Gracie hurried after the small group who surrounded Kordon. Bazteen and Saffron, Kordon's younger brother, had appeared and quickly wrapped Gracie safely between them. He would look for clues here before anyone else could disrupt the scene. He would start with the male he had killed and then the nurse who had betrayed them. He hoped she was still alive, at least until he was finished with her.

Chapter 7

Two weeks later: Pyrus Spaceport

"I swear I'm going to kill her," Froget muttered as he searched another crowded bar. "If I'm going to die anyway, I might as well have a good reason for it. Maybe I'll be lucky and Ti'Death will just shoot me."

"What's that, Frog?" The huge yellow and black bartender asked. "I didn't hear what you wanted."

"My name is Froget! Not Frog, Froget!" Froget growled as he hopped up onto the tall stool. "Have you seen Skeeter?"

Hornet's antennas flickered madly for several seconds before he shook his head. "Gods no! I haven't seen her since she was here a few weeks back. It took me that long to get the rest of the tables repaired. What are you doing with Skeeter?" He asked innocently, not wanting Froget to know he had been the one to recommend him to Ti'Death.

"I need a Reptilian Runner," Froget sighed loudly. "I'm her new co-pilot. Or I was as of yesterday. I'm probably going to be dead tomorrow if I don't find her."

Hornet set a large glass with blue flames burning on the top of it in front of Froget with a look of sympathy. He slapped at a small spill of the flaming liquid with the damp cloth he pulled from his waist before leaning on the bar and looking at Froget with his multiple eyes. He watched as the small green creature blew out the flames and took a long, depressing drink.

"Okay, tell me what she's done now," Hornet said. "You know the life expectancy of her co-pilots have not been long. Well, except for the human one. I think he is still alive."

"Oh, he's alive, just not all in one piece," Froget replied in a discouraged voice. "Five weeks with her and I'm ready to slit my own throat and save her father the trouble."

Hornet threw his head back and a loud buzzing laugh filled the crowded bar. From the look on the small creature's face, he was going to need something a little stronger before the night was over. He knew Ti'Death's reputation, especially when it came to his unusual daughter. While she was human, she was the strangest one he had ever met before. She almost always caused a riot whenever she came in and was totally clueless to the fact she was the cause of it.

The last time she had come in was a little over two weeks before. She had joined in a game of Battle Beasts with a couple of cutthroat pirates from the outer rim that had more credits than brains between the two of them. They had thought the curvy redhead with the innocent smile and flashing eyes would be an easy target in more ways than one.

Hornet had heard the two males talk about taking more than her credits. They planned to enjoy her and thought of ransoming her back to Ti'Death which was suicide in the first place. By the end of the game, she had taken everything but their underclothes.

Enraged, they had accused her of cheating. When one of the men jumped up, so had Skeeter.

Unfortunately, one of the males had just ordered a Reptilian Runner. When she swept her arms forward to gather her winnings, her hand hit the tall glass of flaming liquid igniting the front of the pirate's long leg coverings setting them on fire.

In his panic, the pirate had turned and knocked a serving platter of food onto a group of Bulltian miners. Food covered the thick, massive creatures who surged up in fury. Hornet had watched as Skeeter stuffed the credits down her shirt as the other pirate tried to grab them. She had fallen back into her chair which tipped into another barmaid carrying a pitcher of icy Frozen Moon which flew over a group of Zion warriors. All the Zion warriors saw was the pirate with his hands out as Skeeter was now on the floor.

Hornet had watched as she had crawled under the tables until she made it to the door where she stood up, wiped her hands on her dark blue pants, fluffed her hair and straightened her shoulders leaving a battlefield of flying fists and bodies behind her. A smile curved his lips when he remembered seeing her turn and peek back inside the bar, biting her lower lip before giving him a small apologetic smile. The only thing he could do was call for security to come break up the fighting mass of bodies and clean up the mess. Technically, she hadn't done a thing but beat a couple of pirates at their own game.

"So, what has she done?" Hornet asked, nodding to the other bartender to take over the orders coming in. "Is she in trouble?"

"Is she...," Froget asked in disbelief. "SHE *is* trouble. In three weeks, we have gone to four Spaceports. She has managed to hit one Zion Warship, which she painted a huge pink line down, hit four space markers, rammed one pirate ship and almost crashed into four asteroids. She doesn't have a clue how to fix more than the basics on the *Lulu Belle*. Her idea of repairing something is to take it out and make a sculpture out of it or paint it some awful color. I have had to tape together the thrusters, the navigation module is shot and I have red and black bugs all over my cabin that I want to eat so bad my tongue hurts from trying to taste them!"

"So, where is she now?" Hornet asked, unsure of what to say about the rest.

He remembered Ti'Death's own experience with Skeeter's piloting skills. He had come in more than once the past couple of years and downed half of his supply after taking Skeeter out for 'lessons' when she announced she wanted to work for his freighter line so she could learn the business.

"The girl can't pilot worth a damn. We're on our second freighter in a month," Ti'Death had slurred at him. "She scares the hell out of me. Can't talk and navigate at the same time and forget backing up or docking the damn things."

Hornet had just poured his old friend another drink. He had promised him that he would do what he could to keep Skeeter safe while she was on the Spaceport. He felt a tinge of guilt that he had been the one to suggest Froget as a replacement for Skeeter's last co-pilot, but he thought the small amphibian creature could handle it. Now, he wasn't so sure it had been a fair thing to do to the other male.

Skeeter's last co-pilot had plotted to sell the curvy girl to a brothel. Luckily, Skeeter had mentioned where Druss planned to take her as a surprise to her dad. Ti'Death had been furious and the male had disappeared on his way to the bathroom.

"I don't know. She was gone by the time I woke up. I spent half the night working on the thrusters. I planned to take the navigation module apart and see if I could repair it. I left it on my workbench. When I woke up, Skeeter was gone along with the navigation module," Froget said. "I've checked all the major dealers and they haven't seen her. Ti'Death is going to roast my legs and eat them while I watch. I just know it."

"She'll turn up. She always does," Hornet assured the little green male. "The girl has one of those human angels watching over her."

"She needs a whole army of them. It's the only way they could remain sane," Froget muttered, dropping his head onto the bar. "Pour me another one, Hornet. I need it."

"Red and black bugs, huh," Hornet chuckled.

Froget just groaned and wrapped his hands around his drink. His eyes closed as he quickly blew out the flames and downed the drink. He was going to need a lot more before the night was over.

* * *

Skeeter bit her lip as she walked down the narrow, dark alley. This is where Artemis said she could get the new navigation module. At least, she thought it was where he said she could get it. Was it level one or eleven? God, she sucked when it came to remembering numbers and stuff like that.

I should have just told daddy I'm not a good pilot, she thought. *I should have just told him I wanted to be an artist.*

Instead, she had been too afraid of disappointing him. She really wanted to make him proud of her. If she could only be good at something. She was horrible at maiming and dismemberment. She fainted at the first sign of blood!

She was horrible with numbers and could barely keep track of the balance of credits in her account. She had made a mess when she had tried to work in the firm. She thought if she could pilot one of the freighters that might be fun. After all, she could work on her art between Spaceports and there was always lots of interesting stuff that she could use to create new pieces. What she hadn't taken into consideration was she was lousy at piloting, knew nothing about repairing engines or navigation without instrumentation and before she could get on the Spaceports she had to dock with one which came back to the fact that she was lousy at piloting.

I do love the little space scooters, though, she thought with a sigh. *Those are fun.*

She felt bad about damaging the thrusters again when she hit the pirate ship. She thought Froget might forgive her if she returned with a new navigation module. That hope led her to her current situation.

She snuck out while Froget was still asleep. He had worked all night. She knew because his cussing and the loud banging on the pipes kept waking her up. She thought if she could surprise him with the new module he wouldn't be so upset with her. She hadn't meant to hit the thrusters when the pirate ship came after them. She thought it was the main engines.

Instead of disappearing into the vastness of space, she had stalled the engines when she overcompensated. She had gotten nervous when Froget yelled at her and she didn't do well when she was nervous. She ended up hitting the orange button with the minus on it that meant backwards when she meant to hit the green button that meant go very fast. She thought if she color-coded the buttons different colors it would help her remember what each one did.

Instead, she ended up backing into the front of the pirate ship as they came up behind them. She knew the damage must have been bad because the alarms sounded. Her dad said that alarms in space were not good and she needed to find out what was wrong or get to the escape pod as fast as possible.

Luckily, Froget had been able to turn them off and get them going before the pirates had a chance to board them. Not that it was likely to happen as there had been a huge flash of light behind them before a shockwave had caused more alarms to go off. Froget was able to shut those off too, thank goodness.

"There it is!" Skeeter breathed in relief when she saw a dim flashing light that said Parts.

She hurried forward, pausing to look around before she pushed open the heavy door and stepped inside. She breathed a sigh of relief when she saw the walls were lined with all kinds of parts. There were three men standing inside. One behind the counter and two in front of it.

Skeeter pushed the hood of her cloak back and smiled. "Hi, I need a part for my freighter. Do you mind if I look around for a few minutes?"

Chapter 8

Banshore Spaceport

Krac scowled at the men surrounding him. For the past two weeks he had been following one lead after another. Each one led him a step closer to finding the men who kidnapped Violet. Unfortunately, he was still no closer to finding out who the leader of the New Order was or where he might find him.

The dead male at the medical tower had given him his first clue. While there was no identification on the male, Krac had been able to link him to the Tillman Corporation back on Earth through facial and DNA scans. Tillman was one of the largest suppliers of weapons for the Earth's military.

The founder was also a contributor that funded the research lab that developed him. Richard Tillman had remained free because there had been no trail of paperwork that lead back to him. Krac knew better, but Anastasia made him promise to not go after Tillman as it would prove his point that Krac should have been destroyed instead of set free. Instead, she promised to have him watched so she could bring him down publicly, a fact that caused open hostility between her and Tillman.

Video feeds from the apartment where the nurse lived showed the shadowy face of one of the other males, the one who held Gracie. Krac had finally been able to make a facial match after piecing together numerous images. Harden Blake was a mercenary for hire who was wanted in at least three star systems for the murder of prominent political figures. He had found the nurse dead in one of the exam rooms at the medical center. From the evidence in her apartment, she and Harden had been lovers.

It was the piece of information he had been downloading when Kordon alerted him that had been his first big break. A personal starship belonging to Richard Tillman was requesting emergency clearance to depart from Zion. He had tracked it to Banshore Spaceport. It would appear that his movements were being tracked as well based on his welcoming committee. The only way that was possible was if the sleek starship that Anastasia had commissioned for him had been tagged with a tracker, or worse, there was a traitor within Anastasia's inner circle.

One of the men spit on the ground before grinning at him. He held a long laser whip in his right hand, tapping it against the palm of his left. Krac watched as his eyes ran up and down him with a sneer of contempt.

"You don't look so big and mean for being a monster," he chuckled menacingly. "If you live, we'll see how good you are in the fight rings."

Krac stared intently at the man. He would be the second to die. The man to his back and left would be the first as he held a dart gun. He could process and control being shot better than drugged. If these were Tillman's men, and he was positive they were, then Tillman would have given them the drugs that could neutralize him. He could not take a chance on that. The other four men would die at random.

"Where is Councilman Jefe's daughter? If you tell me, I'll kill you quickly. If you don't, I will make sure I take my time. Believe me, I know many, many ways to prolong your death," Krac said quietly.

"Fill him with a low enough dose he can feel the whip, Sal," the leader of the group ordered. "I want him begging for us to kill his ass."

Krac didn't wait any longer. With a slight shift of his weight, he kicked out backwards. His booted foot caught the man holding the dart gun in the throat, crushing it. He ducked and swiveled, grabbing the dart gun as it fell out of the dying man's hand as he grabbed his shattered throat. Completing the circle on his heel, he fired a dart into the man with the whip. He decided he wanted him alive.

He ejected the second dart in the gun into his hand as he stood up. He swung out with both hands. His right hand smashed the butt of the gun into the third man's jaw while his other drove the tip of the second dart into the fourth man's forehead, piercing his brain.

He grabbed the man whose jaw he had broken and pulled him in front of him as the fifth and final man lifted the laser pistol he had drawn and fired. The man in Krac's arms jerked as his chest was riddled with laser bursts. Krac pulled the laser pistol from the dead man's waist as he let the body fall and fired a single shot between the last man's eyes.

Twirling the pistol in his hand, he tucked it casually into the waistband of his pants before bending and effortlessly throwing the unconscious male over his shoulder. He wanted answers and he was going to get them. The male was about to discover the true meaning of wishing he were dead.

* * *

Skeeter glanced sideways, keeping her eyelashes lowered as she picked up parts that she didn't have a clue what they went to. Since she wasn't sure what the part she needed was called she didn't want to ask the men. Besides, the two at the counter didn't look like they were the kind of men who were very helpful. For that matter, neither did the guy behind the counter.

"We need to make contact. Tell the Leader that the gray bastard is breathing down our necks. We've sent some men to stop him, but if we don't deliver the package soon and disappear, we are in trouble," the meaner-looking of the two said quietly. "We need more men to kill him."

"And help Mace," the larger male growled. "He shot Mace. He needs help."

"Shut up, you moron," the male hissed, glancing at Skeeter, who quickly picked up a long cylinder shaped device. "We need to talk in private."

"Back here," the male behind the counter grunted. "Don't take anything without paying or I'll cut your hands off," he yelled out at Skeeter.

Skeeter looked up at him with wide eyes. "I'm not a thief! I have credits," she replied indignantly.

"Just remember what I said," the male snapped before he jerked his head. "Back here."

Skeeter watched in the reflection of a large piece of metal as the fat yellow male behind the counter unlocked a wide door and pushed the top of the counter up. She breathed a sigh of relief when the men walked through the opening and disappeared through a door behind the counter area.

Now, she could really look for what she needed without worrying if they asked her questions she couldn't answer. She pulled the small part that Froget had removed from the navigation module. Even to her untrained eyes it looked burnt.

She quickly scanned the shelves closest to her before moving to the ones closer to the counter. She stood on her tiptoes, trying to see what was on the top shelf but she was too short. Turning, she scanned the room. Her eyes lit on a small crate with a handle on it.

Skeeter glanced toward the doorway where the men had disappeared before glancing back up at the shelf. It wouldn't hurt to take a quick peek. She hurried over to the crate, deciding she would rather look for herself instead of waiting to ask any of the scary men. She was surprised at how heavy the little crate was considering it looked like it was empty.

She was breathing heavy by the time she set it down next to the shelves. Standing on it, she looked at abundance of parts. She set the broken piece down on the top shelf and ran her hand around over some parts that were closer to the wall. Her hand wrapped around one item that looked similar to what she needed when a small whimper caught her attention.

Skeeter looked over her shoulder, puzzled. She shrugged her shoulders thinking she must be hearing things and was about to turn back to her search when the whimper sounded again. This time, a little louder than the first time.

"Who's there?" Skeeter whispered loudly.

"Mommy?" A tiny voice whimpered. "Mommy, I'm scared."

Skeeter's eyes widen in disbelief when she realized the tiny voice was coming from the crate she was standing on. She scrambled down off of it and knelt on the floor so she could look through the mesh covering one side of the small box. Her breath caught when a pair of vivid green eyes, filled with tears, gazed back at her from a dirty face.

"Oh my," Skeeter whispered. "What are you doing in there?"

"Bad... bad... men... hurt my daddy," the tiny little girl whispered. "They... took me from my mommy. I want to go home. Pretty please. I want my mommy and daddy."

Skeeter's eyes filled with tears as she heard the pitiful plea. Memories of her own parents, now faded by time, flashed through her mind. She reached her fingers through the wire in comfort. Her eyes skirted toward the doorway in the back again.

"How about you come with me?" Skeeter whispered back. "I have a big freighter. I bet we could find your mommy and daddy. It will be like an adventure. You have to be really quiet though, so the bad men don't know."

"Like hide-and-seek?" The little girl asked excitedly. "I like that game. Mommy made Uncle Krac play it with me. He said you have to be really, really quiet. Mom said I'm not supposed to come out until someone says the magic words."

"Ally, ally in come free?" Skeeter responded with a grin.

"You know how to play that game?" The tiny figure asked.

"It's one of my favorites. My dad could never find me," Skeeter giggled. "Let's get you out of here."

The little girl nodded and put her fingers to her lips. Skeeter looked over her shoulder again before quickly undoing the wires holding the mesh closed. She reached in and helped the tiny figure as she crawled out of the small box. Her lips tightened in anger when she saw the dark tracks of dirt where the child had been crying.

"My name's Skeeter," Skeeter whispered as she picked up the tiny body. "What's yours?"

"Violet," she replied, laying her head on Skeeter's shoulder. "I'm hungry."

Skeeter ran her hand down along the girl's thin back and hugged her close. "I'll fix you something as soon as we get back to the *Lulu Belle*."

She turned to leave before she realized that she forgot the part to the navigation system. Tightening her arms around Violet, she stepped up onto the crate and reached for the part she had set down. She quickly slid it back into the pocket of her cloak before jumping down off the crate.

She rolled her eyes when she realized she needed to put the crate back where she found it. She bent down and grasped the now much lighter box and carried it back over to next to the side where she got it. She remembered the man behind the counter telling her not to take anything without paying for it. Deciding since Violet wasn't theirs in the first place, the rule shouldn't apply. Still, it wasn't right to take something without leaving something, even if it wasn't theirs.

She bit her lip and decided she should leave something in exchange for taking Violet so they couldn't say she stole her. She glanced around before deciding she would leave a few credits and her bracelet. Both were worth something. She quickly removed her bracelet and sighed with regret as she had loved the way it turned out and hadn't had it for very long before dropping it through a hole in the top of the crate along with twenty credits.

"What are you doing?" Violet asked, watching Skeeter with a curious expression.

"I left payment for you so they can't say I stole you," Skeeter said with a grin. "I still think I got the better deal."

"Me too," Violet said, yawning and laying her head back down again. "I want my mommy and daddy."

"I know, sweetheart. I missed my mommy and daddy, too," Skeeter whispered. "Now, be as quiet as a mouse."

Skeeter hurried out of the dim store smiling when Violet didn't reply. The precious bundle in her arms was already asleep. She felt a pang of regret that she didn't get the part they needed for the *Lulu Belle* but she was sure that Frog would understand. He had to! There was no way Skeeter could have left the little girl with those horrible men. She shuddered when she remembered what the bad men did to her own family. She wasn't much older than Violet but she could still remember the screams.

Chapter 9

"Are you insane?" Froget asked again as he stared at Skeeter. "Do you have a death wish or something? Do I? I must, for having ever agreed to take on this assignment! If your dad doesn't kill me, you are determined to make sure it happens."

Skeeter paused as she dried Violet's blonde curls. "What does daddy have to do with this?" She asked in confusion.

"Who do you think hired me? I'm supposed to keep you safe! That is an impossible job," he growled.

Skeeter looked down on Violet when she giggled at Frog. "He looks like the frogs in my princess books. If you kiss him will he turn into a prince?" She asked looking up at Skeeter.

Skeeter smiled back down at the beautiful little girl sitting on the counter in their medical bay. They had left the Pyrus Spaceport the moment Frog saw what she had brought back. He had said some extremely colorful words before snapping his mouth shut when she covered Violet's ears and admonished him for his language.

"Unfortunately, no. I already tried that. He stayed the same," she whispered with a wink.

"Are we going to find my mommy and daddy?" Violet asked.

"Of course! We'll find them in no time, won't we Frog?" Skeeter assured her, tucking a wayward curl behind Violet's ear.

"We will be lucky to find the next spaceport! Have you forgotten the navigation system is shot? Without the old module I can't even try to bypass the system," he snorted. "And I told her to never kiss me again. It is dangerous."

"Why is it dangerous?" Violet asked.

"Because males who do end up dead or missing parts of their bodies!" He growled under his breath. "I need to try to figure out a way to fix the navigation system so we know where in the hell we are."

"Oh, I forgot. I do have the old module," Skeeter said, reaching for her cloak that was lying on the bed next to Violet. She pulled the small module out of the pocket and handed it to him before turning and picking Violet up in her arms.

"Froget! I've told you my name is… oh, forget it," he snapped out. "Where did you get this?"

Skeeter looked at his puzzled face in confusion before her eyes dropped to the part in his hand. It was similar to the one she had taken but it wasn't burnt. She sighed when she realized she had just given him another reason to be mad at her.

"Oh darn it! I grabbed the wrong thing. I'm so sorry, Frog!" She said glumly. "I thought it was the one I had left on the shelf."

"No, this is good. I can make this work as long as the star charts stored in it are still good. I've got most of yours backed up, but I wasn't sure if it was complete. I can…."

Skeeter rolled her eyes at Violet causing the little girl to giggle as they both listened to Frog mutter under his breath as he walked away from them. She followed him before turning toward the galley. She was hungry too.

"How about a grilled cheese sandwich?" Skeeter asked.

"What is that?" Violet asked, winding her arm around Skeeter's neck.

"You've never had a grilled cheese sandwich? Tila used to make them for me whenever I was sad. If I was really, really sad she made me macaroni and cheese too. It is an Earth dish. She says it is disgusting, but it isn't," Skeeter promised. "It is the best food in the whole star system."

Violet frowned for a moment before she grinned. "I think I'm feeling really, really sad," she giggled.

"Two macaroni and cheese and grilled cheese sandwiches coming up," Skeeter replied. "I think I'm feeling really, really sad too."

"Why are you sad?" Violet asked in a serious voice.

Skeeter winked at Violet making her giggle again. "Because Frog didn't turn into a handsome prince when I kissed him," she whispered in a dramatic whisper. "It totally broke my heart."

Violet's giggles turned to laughter before she wound both arms around Skeeter's neck and hugged her. "I really, really like you, Skeeter."

Skeeter felt the tug on her heart at the heartfelt words. "I love you too, Violet. We'll find your mommy and daddy. Until then, I'll take care of you just like my Tila took care of me."

"Thank you, Skeeter," the muffled voice said.

"My pleasure, sweetheart," Skeeter said, protectively hugging the small body to hers. "My daddy is going to be so excited to meet you.'

"Is he like you?" Violet asked curiously, looking into Skeeter's dancing blue eyes.

"Have you ever wanted to have your own dragon?" Skeeter asked Violet, waiting until the little girl nodded. "Well, he looks just like the dragons in the picture books only he is a good dragon that will always be there to protect you."

"Oh...." Violet breathed out, her eyes growing huge as she thought of having her own dragon. "Do you think he can be my dragon too?"

"Of course!" Skeeter promised, setting Violet down on the chair in the narrow galley and tickling her. "He's big enough to protect the both of us."

"Just like my daddy and Uncle Krac!" Violet crowed. "They can kick anyone's butt! Mommy said so."

Chapter 10

Krac pressed the eject button on the disposal tube ignoring the hoarse screams coming from it. Within seconds, only the hum of the starship could be heard. The tracking device and the male who had given him the information he wanted now floated in space.

"Connect," he ordered as a communication summons came in.

"Krac, this is Kordon," a dark voice came over the comlink he was wearing. "Where are you?"

Krac was about to respond when he heard Gracie's voice chiding her mate in the background. The warmth filled him again when he heard the hint of steel he was used to hearing in her voice. She would make sure Kordon stayed put until he was healed. He had been in touch with her at least once a day to post updates and find out how her mate was doing.

Kordon had been brought out of the medically induced coma two days before. Since he woke, he had tried to find out Krac's location. He sounded a little stronger today.

"I believe I know where Violet is," he replied, instead. "I will let you know when I have her."

"Damn it," Kordon started to say before his voice faded.

"Kordon, lay back. The healer swore if you tried to get up, she would sedate you again," Gracie said soothingly. "Krac, what have you discovered so far?"

"The threat to you is still there, Gracie," Krac said. "From the information I have just received, there is another planned attack to capture you."

"When?" Gracie and Kordon's voice sounded at the same time. "I swear, Kordon, if you don't stay still I'm going to knock you out. I won't lose you, do you understand. I can't. I need you. Violet needs you."

Krac heard the underlying stress in Gracie's voice. Kordon must have as well as he muttered for her to lay down next to him. He waited as Kordon murmured an apology to Gracie for upsetting her.

"The male did not have an exact time, but there is another plan to kidnap Gracie. They believe Kordon has been killed. I would expect it within the next few days," Krac explained what he had learned from the male he had 'interrogated' at length. "I was able to get a location on the four males from the Medical Tower. I am heading to their location now."

"But, we only saw three males," Gracie said.

"The fourth was operating the skiff they used to escape. Kordon, Richard Tillman is behind Violet's kidnapping. I'm sure of it. They left in his private starship," Krac bit out as a quiet rage burned deep inside him. "Be prepared. The men he sends in will be highly trained and well-armed."

"We will be ready for them," Bazteen's voice called out loudly. "I'll personally kill that son-of-a-bitch. No one harms my family."

"Tillman is mine to kill," Krac said. "Just be prepared. I am heading to Pyrus Spaceport. That is the current location of the starship."

"Krac," Kordon's voice sounded weaker than before over the comlink.

"Yes?"

"Bring my daughter home... please," Kordon's hoarse voice asked. "Whatever it takes, bring her home."

A picture of the laughing green eyes, so like her mother's, formed in his mind. Her shining face as she looked down at him as he held her in the air. His fingers moved to his cheek where she had 'drawn' her pretty pictures with dirty fingers. He blinked several times before storing the image again.

"I will," he said in a voice that sounded suspiciously gruff. "I will."

"Thank you, Krac," Gracie's soft voice said. "Be safe."

Krac disconnected the link. He frowned when he realized that he was still standing outside the disposal tube. A small part of him wished he could retrieve the male he had discharged so he could do it all over again. He wanted each and every member of the New Order to understand that they were on his list for elimination. He wanted them to know what it was like to be hunted. Because he was definitely going to kill everyone involved in Violet Jefe's kidnapping.

* * *

Later that night, Krac held the owner of the small parts shop up by his throat. He had tracked two of the men to the dim, non-descriptive shop through the surveillance system the Spaceport maintained.

Between that and a few well-placed credits, he found the place with no trouble.

"I... don't... know what you are talking about," the massive creature wheezed. "I just sell parts."

Krac raised his hand and drew a thin line between the creature's eyes before he placed the short blade he held between his own teeth and ran his finger along it. He placed his bleeding finger between the creature's eyes. It was the least resistive area on the massive frame and he would be able send the small probes into the male's bloodstream.

His lip curled in distaste as the acidic blood burned the tip of his finger. He ignored the pain, shutting down the nerve-endings long enough to send enough nano-bots to retrieve the information before they were destroyed by the corrosive blood.

"Tell me," Krac bit out.

The massive creature chuckled. "You cannot use your talents on me, assassin. My blood can kill anything."

"So can mine," Krac growled as he sent a command.

The creature's laugh turned into a choked gasp as waves of electrical currents rocked through his brain, making his body stiffen. Krac pushed more of his blood into the cut. He ignored the feeling of metal on flesh that told him that the creature's blood had eaten through the outer layer of flesh covering his skeletal frame.

"They're gone," Pius cried out as another wave hit him. "They left."

"Where did they go?" Krac demanded.

"They are looking for the girl," Pius choked out.

"What girl?" Krac asked, pressing deeper until the metal tip of his finger sank into the meaty flesh.

"The one... the one that took the kid," Pius groaned.

"The child is not with the men who kidnapped her?" Krac asked in disbelief.

Pius tried to shake his head, but it was impossible as the metal rubbed against the outer bone protecting his brain. He had never met a creature in any star system that could survive having his blood on them. That was one reason the Leader had chosen him. The Leader swore that his corrosive blood would protect him from the monster that would come looking for the kid.

"What are you?" Pius asked in pain.

"Who was the woman? What did she look like?" Krac asked instead.

The faint vision of a shadowy figure formed. It was too disjointed for him to get a clear picture. He needed a name, either of the woman or the starship she was on. She must be working with the New Order. She was probably sent to take the child so it would be more difficult for him to track. A low curse escaped him as he realized he was still one step behind those responsible for taking Violet. He would kill the woman as slowly as he had killed every other creature he had encountered so far.

"Don't know her name," Pius whispered. "She said she needed a part. She just wanted a part."

"Do you know what starship she came in on?" Krac asked, pressing the metal tip of his finger deeper.

"Wait! I heard one of the men say she was Ti'Death's daughter. *Lulu Belle*. She is captain of the *Lulu Belle*," Pius forced out as he remembered. "She is…"

Pius never finished his sentence. Krac had enough information. The mysterious and very dangerous Razor-tooth Triterian was involved with the New Order. Krac had heard of Bulldog Ti'Death. The male was extremely wealthy and dangerous. It would appear his daughter followed in her father's footsteps.

He would have to be very careful. He hadn't been joking when he said he would have a hard time defeating a Razor-tooth Triterian. They were massive creatures with layer upon layer of scales that were as strong as the metal that made up his skeletal frame. They could unsheathe claws over a foot long, making it difficult to get close to them. If one was able to get close, they had rows of razor-sharp teeth that could slice through skin and bone with one swipe.

Krac stared at the exposed tip of his finger. With a silent command, tissue began reforming over it. Within seconds, the flesh was once again soft and gray. That was just one of the advancements designed into him over the original Alluthans who would have needed to replace the finger. He glanced at the slumped body of the shopkeeper. Fury burned through him that Violet was exposed to such creatures. Now, she was in a far more terrifying situation.

Yes, he thought as he pulled the hood of his cloak over his head and exited the dim shop. *It would be difficult to kill Ti'Death's daughter, but not impossible. I just hope she has not harmed Violet first.*

Chapter 11

"Ahhhh!" Violet cried out as the sword went through her. "You..." She whispered before her tiny body crumpled to the floor of the corridor.

"Argh!" The large creature growled as it swung its massive head back and forth menacingly as it stepped closer to the still figure. "Roarrrrrr!"

"Will you two knock it off? What in the hell are you supposed to be?" Froget yelled out from the bridge.

Skeeter pushed back the large head of the costume she was wearing so she could see. She moaned when the huge head she was wearing hit the wall and popped her on the end of the nose. She dropped the small, plastic sword in her hand and grabbed her offended appendage.

"I'm a dinosaur," Skeeter said in a muffled voice.

"Are you okay, Skeeter?" Violet asked, sitting up and pulling the other plastic sword out from between her arm and her body.

"I bumped my nose," Skeeter replied. "What to kiss it and make it better?"

Violet's delighted laugh echoed in the passageway leading to the bridge. "You're silly."

Skeeter just grinned before she let out a loud roar and put the mask back on over her head. She laughed as Violet squealed before she jumped up and started running down the corridor. Skeeter did her best to keep up, but it was hard to do in the bulky costume that she had found during one of her many stops.

Froget rolled his eyes and turned back to the freighter controls. He frowned as he thumbed through the unusual star charts that kept popping up. It had been four days since they had left Pyrus. They had floated somewhere between Newport and Banshore Spaceports. Not bad even if that was between one end of the star system and the other. It had taken him a day and a half to finish modifying the module, but it had worked like a charm.

During that time, he had to admit he was thankful that Skeeter had found the little person. It had kept her focused on caring for the child instead of wreaking havoc on the freighter she was supposed to be the captain of. He shook his head in amazement that Ti'Death let his only daughter loose on the universe.

Well, he thought with a sigh. *Maybe I should be more amazed that the universe has survived with her loose in it.*

A loud scream shook him out of his musing. That one was different from the ones he had been hearing for the past few days. His heart raced as he hopped down out of the Captain's chair and took off down the passageway. He turned the corner and froze when he saw a huge gray creature standing in the center of it holding two very long, very dangerous looking curved blades in his hands. One of the long horns from Skeeter's costume lay on the floor behind him.

* * *

Krac had been surprised and more than a little suspicious at how easy it had been to board the huge, pink freighter. At first, he had thought he was seeing things when he had gotten his first visual of the *Lulu Belle*. It wasn't just pink. It was a blazing hot pink with flowers on it!

The only thing that Krac could determine was that Ti'Death's daughter must be so sure of her ability to kill anything that came at her that she wasn't afraid to flaunt it. No one else that he knew would be caught dead in such a ship! He had opened the emergency access underneath the freighter and came up through one of the large storage bays. From the looks of her cargo, or lack of it, she mustn't even be trying to pretend to be a legitimate freighter pilot. Most short haul freighters made sure they had a full cargo before heading to their next destination. It was the only way to either break even or make a marginal profit if they wanted to stay in business.

He had quickly accessed the computer system. He wanted to connect to the PLT, or Personal Location Trackers, that were standard for all commercial freighters to locate those aboard the ship in cases of emergency. He was confused when he discovered there were no operational PLT's. He decided that Ti'Death's daughter must have dispensed with them since this was not a genuine freighter operation but a cover for her true occupation – mercenary for hire.

His heart beat heavily when he heard Violet's terrified scream and the loud, muffled roar of the Razor-tooth Triterian. He had rounded the corner in time to see Violet's small body fly through an open doorway, the creature just steps behind her. The only thing that saved Gracie and Kordon's daughter was the Triterian was too large to fit through the door.

He roared out in rage as it tried to work its way into the room, clawing at the sides. Violet's loud screams filled the narrow passageway and fueled his determination to kill the beast. He swung his blades at the same time as the creature, sensing his approach, turned and emitted a bloodcurdling cry of attack. Krac's eyes narrowed when another creature suddenly appeared.

"What the… who are you and how did you get on board the *Lulu Belle*?" Froget demanded.

"He cut off one of my horns!" Skeeter cried out, lifting her hand to touch where the horn on the top of the costume was missing.

Krac reacted the moment the Triterian moved, slicing through the air at the arm that was rising up. He knew they could extend additional razor-sharp scales in defense. He was shocked when the arm fell to the floor as well, leaving a huge gaping dark hole. The creature squealed again and stumbled backwards.

"Frog!" Skeeter cried out in terror.

Krac watched as the small amphibian creature named Frog pulled two small blades from his waist. The male jumped up, ricocheting off the left wall and over the Triterian where it landed between her and him. He turned as the male released his long, sticky tongue at him.

"Stay back or I'll kill you," Frog snarled.

Krac evaluated the threat of the other male. He had already classified him and pulled up all known information. All data coming back indicated the male was of negligible threat. No, his biggest threat was from the Triterian who could take out three Zion warriors at one time.

"Move," Krac demanded. "I will kill you quickly after I have dealt with the Triterian."

"Why do you want to kill me?" A soft, confused voice asked. "What did I do?"

Krac ignored the warmth that flooded him at the sound of the husky feminine voice. It must be another ploy. He had never fought a female Triterian before. They must be able to use their voices as well to affect their prey.

"What have you done to her?" Krac growled in a low dark voice, taking a step forward.

"I told you to stay back," Frog snapped.

Krac swung the curved blade in his left hand down at the same time as the creature struck out with his own knife. He felt the sting of the small blade as it cut a long, deep line across his thigh. His own blade neatly cut through the other blade. The creature fell backwards into the Triterian causing it to lose its balance.

"Now, you die," he said coldly, taking a step forward.

"No!" The female Triterian cried out, scrambling up and over the body of the smaller male. "You can't kill him!"

"What in the...?" Krac's voice died as a slender arm popped out of the section of the arm he had cut off.

He watched in disbelief as the slender hand, the same as Anastasia and Gracie's, pushed at its large red head. He stepped backwards when the head fell forward onto the floor and rolled, stopping face up at his feet. His eyes rose from the decapitated head, following the floor where it had rolled until he came to the large, clawed feet. His eyes continued to move up the body of the Triterian until they locked on a pair of vivid blue eyes framed by flaming red hair.

"Oh no," the voice whispered as those amazing blue eyes widened in shock as they stared back at him. "You're bleeding."

Krac looked down at his bleeding leg and sent a command for the skin to heal. He glanced up at the same time as the eyes staring back at him fluttered close and the female collapsed back onto the male who was struggling to get up. He took a step to catch her at the same time as another figure peeked out from behind the door.

"Uncle Krac!" Violet squealed before her eyes flew to the pile of bodies in the corridor. "What did you do to Skeeter? She's my new friend."

Chapter 12

Krac stared at the still figure on the bed. The creature lying on the soft covers was totally different than what he had first encountered in the corridor. He had stood frozen in confusion as the male finally wiggled out from under the massive body that had collapsed on top of him.

It had taken another minute before he understood what the male was ordering him to do. His eyes had been locked on the pale face with its perfectly formed features. A delicate oval face, framed by rich, vibrant red hair touched with strands of gold held him mesmerized. Her lashes lay like fragile crescents against milky white skin. Narrow eyebrows, the same color as her hair, swept over her closed lids like the feathers of a rare cardinal back on Earth. Her nose was small and her lips….

Krac's eyes moved to the softly parted lips of the female as she breathed. They were full and pink. A small smile tugged at the corner of his mouth. Not quite as pink as her ship, but close.

He glanced around the room that Froget, her co-pilot, had ordered him to carry her into and lay her down. It matched the female on the bed. It was bright, colorful yet soft and delicate at the same time.

The walls were a soft blue with white trim. Shelves had been mounted along one wall. Hundreds of different miniature sculptures were on it. The ceiling was lined with twinkling lights and colorful glass, in the shapes of moons, suns and stars, hung from it, catching the light. Even her bed wasn't immune to her feminine touch. Several meters of shimmering gray cloth hung from the ceiling like a curtain around it.

He carefully picked up her right hand, turning it in his large palm as he studied the slender fingers. A colorful ring with strange symbols etched into it encircled her thumb. He rubbed his own thumb over it absent-mindedly as he thought back to what had happened earlier.

* * *

He remembered staring down at the unconscious female in puzzlement. Her faint words of him bleeding had momentarily distracted him. When he looked up, she was collapsing on top of the Goliath Amphibian. He had watched, frozen, as the small, greenish male finally crawled out from under her and stood up, staring at him in disgust.

"Well, are you going to kill us or are you going to help me get her up? She'll be out for at least a good twenty minutes," Froget had growled at him. "This is the last bloody thing I need right now."

"Is Skeeter sick?" Violet asked, looking back and forth from Frog to Krac with tears in her eyes. "We were just playing, Uncle Krac. It was her turn to be the monster."

"She's not sick," Froget grunted as he yanked on the bottom half of the costume. "She can't stand the sight of blood. She passes out. The first time it happened was when she cut her finger in the galley. Scared the shit out of me. I..." he grunted again and fell on his ass as the legs of the costume finally pulled free. "I make her wear gloves now when she is chopping things up."

"Oh," Violet said, watching with wide eyes. "But, she isn't sick?"

"No, kid. She's not sick," Froget responded again. "Listen, I don't know who in the hell you are or how you got on the *Lulu Belle* but if you aren't going to kill us can you at least help? Otherwise I'll have to either leave her here or drag her ass down to her cabin. In case you haven't noticed, no one is piloting this freighter and the auto-pilot doesn't work. We could run into a damn moon any moment as far as I know. The star charts are all screwed up right now so I'm not sure where in the hell we are."

"I will take her. Where is her cabin?" Krac said, bending down and quickly removing the rest of the costume.

"I can show you!" Violet said with a happy smile now that she knew Skeeter wasn't sick. "I've been sleeping there too. Skeeter said it would be better in case I needed any... any stuff. Skeeter says..."

Krac followed Violet as she led him down the long corridor, telling him all the things that 'Skeeter says'. It would appear Skeeter said a lot of things to the impressionable little girl including that they were on an adventure to find her parents. They had made up a game of it while Frog, who grumbled a lot, but was really very funny and nice, tried to fix the ship.

Krac started when he felt slender fingers curl around his. He blinked several times as his eyes focused on the pair staring back at him. He was startled by the sudden heat that engulfed him. This was nothing like what he felt when he looked at Gracie or Anastasia. This was hotter, richer, and more intense than anything he had ever felt before.

A slight tinge of color darkened his skin as he realized that his cock was also reacting to that heat. THAT had never happened when he was around Anastasia or Gracie. For that matter, it had never happened around any female, including the one that had been sent to him in the lab to see how he would react when sexually stimulated. He had found nothing appealing about the heavily made-up female who smelled of stale perfume, sweat and other men.

This one, this female did not smell like any of those things. She smelled like flowers and freshness. The more he thought about it, the harder he grew. He started to pull his hand away, but stopped when she tightened her fingers around it.

"Hi," she whispered with a slightly uncertain smile. "I'm Skeeter."

"I know," Krac replied stiffly, unsure of what else to say.

"Oh. How?" She asked, tilting her head.

"Violet said your name… many times," he admitted a little bemused. "She likes you."

"I like her too," Skeeter replied. "So, what is your name and why did you want to kill me?"

* * *

Deep down, Skeeter knew she should be terrified of the unusual male holding her hand. After all, he had threatened to kill her. Hell, he had even tried.

She figured if he really wanted her dead, he could have done it when she fainted. It was a bad habit of hers whenever she saw blood. One of the healers her dad brought in the first time it happened said it was probably a reaction to a bad memory. He was right. Every time she saw blood, she saw her parents and the other members aboard the small research shuttle lying in pools of it. She remembered scrambling away from it, afraid if it touched her, she would be like them.

When she started to surface, she usually had a panic attack, but this time she hadn't been scared. She liked the feel of the warm hand holding hers. It made her feel – safe. The soft caress along her thumb had made her hungry for more.

She had stared up into the dark gray face of the male, admiring his sharp features. He wasn't 'handsome' like Terry had been. His face had a harder, leaner look to it. His black hair was cut short and hung down just a little over his forehead. He had dark eyes, almost as black as his hair. His nose was long and narrow and his lips, well, they just looked perfect for kissing. She wondered what he would do if she were to kiss him, just to see what it was like.

She didn't like it when a small frown darkened his features. She wanted to see him smile. He didn't look like he smiled much. Smiling was good for a person. It made all the bad things in the world a little less scary when someone smiled. Perhaps he didn't have anyone to smile with. Her dad always said he never smiled or laughed until she came into his life. That was her magic, he told her. She brightened the world around her. Skeeter decided that the man holding her hand needed a little brightness in his world.

Her fingers tightened around his when he started to pull away. She wasn't ready to let him go. In the back of her mind, she was still afraid of the memories that haunted her when she first woke.

"I don't like blood," she murmured. "It makes me faint."

"Yes, that is what the other male said," he replied stiffly.

"I'm sorry about that," she said, looking up at him. "Did you get your leg taken care of while I was out?"

He cleared his throat and shifted in the narrow chair he had pulled up next to the bed. She tightened her fingers around his when he tried to pull his hand away. Instead, she took up the rhythm of running her finger back and forth over his. She tilted her head when she saw his cheeks turn a slightly darker color as she caressed him.

"It is healed," he responded in a slightly deeper, bemused voice. "Violet likes you. She was worried. She showed me where to bring you. Your co-pilot took her to get nourishment. She was hungry. She said I had to sit with you until you were better."

Skeeter smiled when she thought of the beautiful little girl she had rescued. "I like her too. So what is your name and why did you want to kill me?"

"You took Violet," he stated, pulling his hand away from her and standing up. "Why?"

Skeeter sighed at the loss of his warmth and sat up. She swung her legs over the side of her bed. The room tilted for a moment before righting itself. A nervous smile curved her lips when she found herself suddenly at eye level with the huge male as he knelt in front of her, bracing her arms.

"Because," she murmured in a hushed whisper as she leaned forward.

"Because… why?" He asked confused.

"Because I couldn't leave her behind. I want to kiss you," she said, unaware that she said the last part out loud.

"What?" Krac's head jerked back slightly as her words resonated through him. He froze when he felt her hands move up, first to his shoulders, then to the back of his head. "What are you…?"

His words died as Skeeter gently touched her lips to his. They felt just as good as she thought they would. She brushed the tip of her tongue along the seam as her hands tightened in his hair, forcing him off balance so that he fell into her. His breathing increased. The moment his lips parted, Skeeter deepened the kiss.

This… she thought as warmth filled her. *This is what it should feel like when you kiss the right person.*

She moaned when she felt his hands tighten on her arms as he pulled away from her. She reluctantly brushed her lips across his once more before she let him break the contact between them. Her eyes fluttered as she tried to focus back on where they were.

"Why did you do that?" He demanded harshly. "Do you think to make a fool out of me? I could kill you before you take another breath."

Skeeter shivered as he rose and stepped away from her. His face was flushed and his eyes were twin flames of burning coal as he stared down at her. He clenched and unclenched his fists several times before he turned on his heel.

"I am taking Violet," he snapped out over his shoulder as he walked out of her cabin.

Chapter 13

Skeeter scrambled off the bed as the strange man disappeared. She didn't understand what just happened. She could feel the waves of suppressed rage coming off of him. She had kissed a lot of men looking for her Prince Charming. Hell, she had thought Terry had been it until he disappeared on her and joined the monks on Cramoore. She was glad now that he had because his kisses never affected her the way the one she just had did.

"Wait a minute!" She yelled as she hurried down the corridor after him. "Please, will you just wait a second?"

She barely had time to put her hands up to stop herself from plowing into his back when he suddenly stopped. She bit back a groan as she felt the taunt muscles under his shirt. She swore her nerve-endings were about to short circuit from wanting to explore his broad back.

"You can't take Violet!" She said desperately.

She gasped and would have fallen when he turned suddenly on his heel and glared down at her if he hadn't grabbed her wrists that were still up in the air. She looked up at him, trying to think of what she could say to make him stay for just a little longer. Hell, she didn't even know his name yet.

"Why?" He demanded.

"Because," she started to say.

He glared down at her. "The last time you said that you kissed me. What do you want? And why should I not take Violet."

"You can't take her because I don't know your name," Skeeter whispered. "I don't know where you plan to take her. I don't know if you are going to kill me and Frog. You can't take her because I don't... I don't want you to go yet," she finished barely above a whisper.

"Why?" He asked gruffly.

"Why what?" Skeeter asked, confused.

"Why did you kiss me?" He demanded in a strained voice. "Why do you not want me to go?"

Skeeter bit her lower lip again and gave him a small uncertain smile. "I don't know."

Krac scowled fiercely at her response. "You don't know why you kissed me or you don't know why you don't want me to go?" He growled.

Skeeter thought about their conversation for several long seconds before she threw her head back and laughed. It was the strangest, weirdest conversation she had ever had and she loved it. It matched her feelings and what was happening and she suddenly felt wild and free.

She threw her arms around the neck of the huge male standing in front of her when he started to turn away. Standing on her tiptoes, she leaned her forehead against his when he lowered his head to frown down at her. Her lips twitched as she realized she liked it when his large warm hands slid around her waist.

"Can we start over?" She whispered, looking into his eyes. "My name is Lulu Belle Mann. Everyone calls me Skeeter, though. This is my short haul freighter. It isn't big. It isn't fancy, but it is mine. I'd like to welcome you aboard."

Krac stared back into the suddenly serious blue eyes that were gazing intently at him. The fire that had started back in her cabin ignited into a blazing inferno. He swore it felt like the ice around his heart was melting.

"My name is Krac," he finally responded. "Has anyone ever told you that you are a very strange and unusual female?"

A shy smile pulled her lips up at the corners. "Maybe once or twice," she replied in amusement. "But I like strange and unusual. Normal is highly overrated and boring."

Krac frowned. "Why did you kiss me?"

"Because," she whispered, lowering her eyes to his lips. "I wanted to see if your lips tasted as good as they looked."

Krac's hands tightened on her waist, pulling her closer as she leaned into him. His lips sealed over hers in a fierce kiss meant to frighten her away. Instead, a low groan escaped them both as something deep inside them connected.

"Oh no. Oh hell no! Oh, double hell no," a high-pitched voice snapped out breaking them apart. "Your father was very, very clear, Skeeter! He said 'no men, no space, protect at all cost'! He was very, very clear about no men! Of any kind! You are going to get me killed. I just know it. We're in the middle of space and you have to find one of the things that is guaranteed to get me killed!"

Skeeter bit her lip and blushed when she saw Violet staring at her with her little mouth hanging open. She must have been with Frog because she was wearing a small cloth tool belt around her waist and had her plastic sword in it. Skeeter glanced up at Krac who was looking down at her co-pilot like he would like nothing better than to step on him.

"Frog, this is Krac. He is…" Skeeter paused as she glanced up at Krac again. "Why are you here again?"

"You're standing in the middle of the corridor kissing the male who thirty minutes ago was going to kill you... us… and you don't even know why he is on your freighter?" Frog asked in outraged disbelief. "And my name is not Frog! It is Froget!"

"I have come to take Violet back to her parents," Krac stated with a raised eyebrow. "She was taken from them."

"By the two men in the shop?" Skeeter asked, curious.

"What do you know about them?" Krac scowled as he turned his gaze back to her. He bit back a silent curse when he couldn't keep his eyes from shifting to her swollen lips. "Where are they?"

Skeeter shrugged. "Not here, thank goodness. They were totally mean looking."

"What were you doing in that shop in the first place?" Krac asked, stiffening as he thought of the danger she must have been in. "Who do you work for?"

"I'm hungry!" Violet's voice suddenly broke the tense atmosphere at Krac's sharp questions. "I'm feeling really, really sad, Skeeter. Can I have macaroni and cheese and a cheesy sandmidge?"

Skeeter's eyes broke contact with Krac's and softened as she saw the hopeful look on Violet's face. She knelt down on one knee and opened her arms. She lifted Violet in her arms and pressed a kiss to her cheek.

"You look absolutely miserable," Skeeter agreed with a wink. "I think you need a big helping of macaroni and cheese to make you feel better."

"And the cheesy sandmidge? I need the cheesy sandmidge too," Violet said with a grin.

"With lots of cheesy in it," Skeeter promised.

She turned and walked toward the galley leaving Krac and Frog to follow if they wanted. Violet didn't deserve to be upset by what was going on. It wasn't her fault that grownups made such a mess out of life. She also didn't want Violet to have to remember what she had been through. She would tell Krac everything she knew but not in front of Violet. She wanted to shield the innocence in the little girl's eyes for as long as possible, just like Bulldog had done for her.

"You know what? I miss my daddy," Skeeter said as she set Violet down. "Would you like to say hi to him after we eat?"

"Can I call my mommy and daddy too?" Violet asked as she stood on the chair so she could watch Skeeter as she prepared their dinner. "I miss my mommy and daddy too."

Skeeter glanced over her shoulder and smiled warmly at Violet as she watched their meal cook in the replicator. Her eyes collided with Krac's for a moment as she waited to see his response to Violet's innocent request. She smiled her thanks when he sharply nodded.

"Yes, baby. We can contact your mommy and daddy too. I know they must miss you something fierce," Skeeter said, wrapping her arm around Violet and lowering her into the seat so she could place the food in front of her.

"Something fierce. Something fierce. My mommy and daddy miss me something fierce," Violet sang in an off-key voice.

Skeeter ran her hand over the wild curls even as she felt the tug on her heart that this little bit of sunshine would soon be with someone else. For a moment, she understood what Bulldog meant when he said the world was a little bit brighter.

Maybe one day she would have her own little girl to make cheesy sandmidges and macaroni and cheese for. Her eyes moved to the huge gray male who stood off to the side of the door, staring at her almost like he could read her mind. He nodded briefly before turning and leaving her and Violet alone to enjoy their meal. Skeeter's heart beat heavily as she thought about the fact that the little girl wasn't the only thing she was about to lose.

If I'm not careful, it will be my heart as well, she thought as she listened to Violet tell her about playing hide-and-seek with her Uncle Krac and other tales.

Chapter 14

"Krac, have you found her?" Kordon asked, leaning forward to pierce Krac with his dark blue eyes.

"She is safe. I have her," Krac replied as he leaned back in the cockpit of his own starship.

"Oh God! Oh God! Oh Kordon!" Gracie's voice broke as she wrapped her arms around her mate from behind and lowered her head to his shoulder. "She's safe. Our little girl. Oh Kordon, she's safe."

Kordon's throat worked furiously as he pulled Gracie around and into his arms. He lowered his head for a moment as he fought for his own self-control. When he looked back up, a cold ruthlessness had filled them.

"Where are you? I can have a warship meet you. Both Ty and Malik are on standby, as well as Bran," Kordon stated.

"I'll send you our current location now," Krac replied.

"Is she… is she okay?" Gracie asked in a husky voice. "Did they hurt her?"

"She is very well. It would appear her kidnappers were not expecting someone else to take their prize," he replied dryly.

"Who?" Kordon bit out even as he notified both of his younger brothers about the location of the short haul freighter.

"She was taken by Captain Lulu Belle Mann," Krac replied.

Kordon frowned. "I've heard that name before."

"She is Ti'Death's daughter, though I do not know how that is possible," Krac answered.

Kordon's face cleared as he recognized the second name. "Now I remember. Rorrak couldn't walk straight for two days after he met her at one of the bars. I had to bail him, Bran and Cooraan out of the brig on Newport. I remember them saying something about Ti'Death's daughter, dancing and a fight that broke out. I'll have to ask them what happened again."

"Can we talk to Violet?" Gracie interrupted. "Please… I need to see that she is alright."

"I'll connect to the *Lulu Belle's* communication system so you can see and speak with her," Krac said.

He focused for a moment as he linked into the *Lulu Belle's* computer system. He found the necessary codes and bypassed the security system so that he had control. He opened the link within seconds. Froget's smooth green head and face appeared on the vidcom.

"What in the hell? What are you doing now? I thought you had left. You need to before Ti'Death finds out you kissed his daughter! He'll have both of us either in that damn tank of his or as new members of Cramoore. Personally, I'll take the tank before I let those bastards cut off my…," Froget's voice faded as he saw the fierce expression on Kordon's face. "That's it! We're dead. She's brought the whole damn Zion council down on us now. I knew I should have stayed in the swamp and been a mushroom harvester. I just knew it."

"Where is my daughter?" Kordon demanded.

"Daddy!" A voice in the background squealed. "It's my daddy! He's here."

"Violet?" Gracie called out, desperate to see her daughter. "Violet, sweetheart."

"Mommy!" Violet's vivid dark green eyes, shimmering with excitement, suddenly appeared on the vidcom. "Hi mommy. I'm on an... an... adventurer. Skeeter and I was playing dinosaurs and knights and I got to be a knight but she was the dinosaur and she was going to eat me up but she hit her nose and she wanted me to kiss it then Uncle Krac came and he cut up her costume and she fell asleep cause he was bleeding then he kissed her all better but I told her I was really sad so she made me cheesy sandmidges and macaroni and cheese. I like it. Can I have some when I come home, even if I'm not sad. Skeeter says her Tila made it for her when she was little."

"Violet," Kordon said, sitting forward as a relieved smile tugged at his lips.

"Oh, Skeeter likes to wear pants too, and Frog doesn't like his name and he isn't a Prince Charming cause Skeeter kissed him and he didn't change, but she hoped he would because he looked just like the frogs in the picture books but he didn't and..."

"Violet Coraleen Jefe," Gracie said sternly. "Take a deep breath." Violet stopped and drew in a big breath. "Now, release it. I love you, Violet. We'll be with you soon."

"I love you too, mommy. I love you, daddy," Violet said, leaning forward and pressing her lips against the screen. "Bye-bye."

"Bye-bye, baby," Gracie whispered, reaching out to touch the screen where Violet's lips had been. "Krac. Thank you."

"I owe you more than I can ever repay," Kordon added gruffly.

"My job is not finished yet," Krac said, disconnecting his connection with the *Lulu Belle* so he could speak privately with Kordon. "The threat is still there. They did not get Gracie this time, but they will try again. We already know that. There is no guarantee that they will not try to take Violet or your son or another family member. They have done this to others on the council back on Earth. More often than not, those members were found too late."

* * *

Harden glanced back at Crane and nodded. Moss stood to the side, his head down as Crane released the box containing Mace. His face twisted in grief and rage as the outer door closed again. He looked up at Harden with dark eyes.

"I am going to kill the gray man," Moss swore. "He killed Mace. I am going to kill him."

"You go right ahead and kill him," Harden responded. "But, we need to get the kid back before they hand her over to one of the warships."

"I have a lock on their location," Crane said. "Are you sure about this? I've got a bad feeling."

"Yes," Harden and Moss said at the same time.

"I've never failed a job and I have a score to settle with the bitch who took the kid. I don't like it when someone steals from me," Harden said.

Crane couldn't help the retort that escaped. "She paid you for her," he reminded the other man. "Fifty credits and a bracelet. You know, if you kill Ti'Death's daughter, he is going to come after you. I've heard he is very protective of her."

Harden's eyes flashed with cold fury. "Then he should have taught her to keep her hands off of other people's merchandise. I don't give a fuck whose daughter she is. She is dead."

"I want to kill the gray man," Moss said again. "You kill the girl. I kill the gray man who killed Mace."

Crane threw his hands up in the air. "Fine! You kill the girl. Moss kills the gray man. I just want to get the fuck out of this alive and richer."

"Then you'd better make sure while we are doing the killing, you get the kid," Harden replied. "Let's get this fucking job done once and for all."

Chapter 15

"So, you're staying?" Skeeter asked quietly as she stepped into the galley later that night. "Until when?"

"There are three Zion warships headed this way," Krac said, looking up from the tablet he held in his hand. "When they arrive and have Violet Jefe in their protection, then I will leave."

Skeeter bit her lip and shifted from one foot to the other. He hadn't really answered her question about how long that would take and she really wanted to know how much time she had before he left. She didn't understand why, but she wanted to know more about him.

"Would you like a drink?" She asked, nervously twisting her hands together when he looked back up at her again. "I'd like a drink and it is only polite to offer. I mean, since I'm getting one and you're sitting here and…. I'll just get you a drink."

Krac's lips twitched as he watched her turn quickly and walk over to the counter. His eyes greedily roamed over her lush figure as she stretched to get a couple of cups out of the cabinet above her head. She was built differently from Anastasia and Gracie. She had wider hips that made his hands itch to hold them. He bit back a groan when she bent to pull a container out from under a lower cabinet.

He quickly schooled his features to a calm mask when she glanced over her shoulder and gave him a shy smile. He closed his eyes the moment she turned back around and breathed deeply. If she didn't quit biting her lower lip, he was going to kiss her again.

He glanced blindly down at the tablet in his hand. He was trying to clean up the mess that she called a security system. He'd had a long talk with Froget while Skeeter was bathing Violet and putting her to bed. He had to agree with the little male; Ti'Death needed to be shot for letting his beautiful but naïve daughter out of his sight.

..*

"She's got a heart of gold that gets her in trouble," Froget had told him soberly as he worked on the auto-pilot. "I don't know why she wants to be a freighter captain. She can't pilot one worth a damn. That's why she's got all the buttons color coded, it's to help remind her what they are supposed to do. On top of that, she is constantly volunteering to haul stuff for free or minimum cost. The only reason we weren't overtaken by pirates a few weeks ago is because she got nervous and backed the freighter into them. I've never seen that happen in open space before."

"She… pirates?" Krac had muttered. "What else?"

"I'm her fifth co-pilot. I think," Froget said glumly. "You don't say no when Bulldog asks you to do something. Especially when the last co-pilot is floating in a freeze tank behind him when he does."

"What happened to her other co-pilots?" Krac asked carefully as he connected with her defense systems. He grimaced when he saw most were offline or deactivated. "Why did Ti'Death kill him?"

"Which one? Druss? He was going to sell Skeeter to one of the brothels run by Ti'Death's arch enemy," Froget said, hissing when sparks flew out of the panel. "Still, I'd rather be dead than have what happened to co-pilot number three," he added with a shudder.

"What happened to the others?" Krac asked again, wishing the man was still alive so he could kill him.

"Well, co-pilot number one was drunk and had taken on cargo that was highly volatile. He didn't correctly secure it down in the cargo bay. You may have noticed the large red bird on the side of the freighter. Skeeter painted it as a symbol of flight when one of the canisters broke loose and blew as they were coming into Sallas. There was a hole the size of a Zion battle tank in the side. The freighter was in planet-side dry dock for three months to repair the damage. The kicker was her co-pilot took the escape pod and fled, leaving Skeeter to bring the freighter in on her own. No one knows how she managed that."

"And number two?" Krac asked, clenching his jaw to keep the curses from escaping.

"Oh, Bulldog killed him after Skeeter told him about the private dance he asked her to give at Zemora's dance club. It seems that he offered Skeeter to three Zion warriors with the promise of a private dance at the exclusive men's club, if you know what I mean. What he didn't know was that she was into studying some ancient Maori Haka Earth dance called The Dance of Life." Froget grinned at Krac. "I saw a vidcom of her doing it. I don't recommend ever asking her. It scared the hell out of me. She is dangerous with a stick. I heard she almost knocked the balls off of one of the men and knocked the other two out before they knew what was happening."

Krac's mouth tightened when he thought about three other males who needed to be killed. Bran, Cooraan and Rorrak forgot to mention that little fact in their story. He gritted his teeth when he thought of what the last male must have done.

"And co-pilot number three?" Krac bit out darkly. "What did he do? What was he killed for?"

Froget looked up in surprise at Krac. "Oh, Terry isn't dead, but he probably wishes he was," he replied. "He is now a monk on Cramoore."

Krac grimaced. He had heard of what happened to the males who went there. The planet was one of the smallest in the star system and had a complete male population of eunuchs.

"What did he do?" Krac asked, wanting to know what the male could have done that was worse than what the others had done. "Try to kiss her?"

"Oh no, something much worse," Froget replied as he slid the cover back over the opening in the panel. "He became Skeeter's lover in the hopes of tapping into Bulldog's bank account."

Froget cursed and looked around frantically when all the lights on the control panel started flashing wildly and the main lights dimmed. He quickly pulled the cover he had just tightened down back off. He looked up to ask Krac if he had any idea of what might have happened as everything returned to normal but the huge gray man was gone.

"Must have been a short somewhere," Froget muttered under his breath with a shrug. "Hope it doesn't happen again."

* * *

Now, as he watched her prepare them something to drink, he couldn't help but be angry at the thought of another male touching her. He looked down again as she carefully picked up the tray she had placed the drinks on and carried it over to the table. He had no right to be angry. It was true, she had kissed him, but it was probably more out of curiosity of what it was like to kiss a monster than out of true desire. This is what the whore the scientists brought in told him.

"I hope you like tea," she said, setting a steaming cup in front of him. "Be careful, it is hot."

"Why did you kiss me earlier?" Krac asked, tilting his head as she sat down across from him.

He watched as her eyes grew wide before her cheeks turned almost as red as her hair. He hadn't meant to ask that question but he couldn't forget the kiss. He could still taste her on his lips. He... liked it.

"I don't know," she finally answered in a soft voice. "I just wanted to."

Krac frowned at her and sat forward. "Do you always do what you want?"

"No, not always," she said, looking away.

Krac's frown deepened when he heard the sadness in her voice. He didn't like it. He liked it when she was laughing; like she did when she was with Violet. He liked it when she smiled as well.

"Are you sad because of the male called Terry? He wasn't interested in you. He was only interested in Ti'Death's credits. Why would you be sad for such a male when it is obvious he never cared about you?" He asked, staring at her.

"I… You… Terry…. That is the most horrible thing anyone has ever said to me!" She whispered in shock as she stood up. "Who told you about Terry? Never mind! It is none of your business," she hissed out, leaning over the small table. "I wish now I had never kissed you! To think I thought you were cute. You… you are not cute any longer and the sooner you are off of my freighter the better!"

Krac's heart twisted as her eyes filled with unshed tears. He had said something to put them in her eyes. Something that was very, very wrong. Frustration ate at him as she pushed away from the table, spilling a little of her untouched tea and turned away from him. His eyes followed her as she hurried out of the galley.

He growled out a curse and stood up. Tossing the small tablet on the table, he rounded it determined to follow her and find out what he had said wrong. He glanced down the corridor frowning when he saw that it was empty. She couldn't have gone very far.

He started down the corridor toward the bridge rationalizing that she would have gone there since she was the Captain. Froget shook his head when he asked him if he had seen her. He spent the next hour searching from one end of the freighter to the other before finally heading back toward her cabin again. She hadn't been in it the first time he checked.

He strode down the long corridor until he was outside her room. The door was still open and the twinkling lights hanging from the ceiling were on. His eyes moved to the open door leading to the bathroom, but only the dim emergency light glowed from it.

His eyes swept the room, pausing on the small body curled up in the bed. Violet was surrounded by small cloth animals in all different shapes and sizes. Her tiny arms were wrapped around a dark red Triterian.

He blinked several times before looking carefully around Skeeter's bedroom. This time when he looked, he tried to see it through her eyes. As he ran his eyes over it, details that he had ignored the first time became clearer.

The walls were painted with beautiful images. The more he stared at them, the more detail emerged. Bright colors were mixed with more subtle shadows as the different worlds she had visited came to life. He looked at the wall that was filled with hundreds of small sculptures. He glanced back at Violet, who was sound asleep before walking over to the wall and picking up one of the delicate pieces.

"A Flying Sea Dragon," he murmured as he recognized the shape of the tiny replica of the small creatures on Sallas.

He turned the piece over and over in his hand, admiring the attention to detail and the accuracy of the body in flight. He set it back on the shelf before he picked up another and then another and then another.

Each piece was painstakingly carved and painted. Some had tiny jewels for eyes while others were just painted. He felt like they were staring back at him.

The last piece he picked up was of a Razor-tooth Triterian. He recognized the features of Bulldog in the miniature. He rolled it in his palm with a deep frown.

"Most people think of him as a monster," Skeeter's voice said softly from the doorway.

Krac slowly turned to look at her. He could see that her eyes were puffy and her lashes were still damp from her tears. He stood still as she walked toward him and gently took the sculpture out of his hand.

"But you didn't?" He asked quietly.

Skeeter smiled at the figure of her 'dad'. "No, never. While others saw his scary teeth and sharp claws, I saw my own personal dragon come to save and protect me. He was larger than life and the most beautiful creature I had ever seen," she said with an uneven smile. She laughed quietly as tears filled her eyes again. "He still is. He's my hero and he always will be," she admitted, looking up at him.

He reached over and carefully picked the sculpture up and set it back on the shelf before turning back to her. He wasn't sure what to do or say so he didn't do either. He just looked down at her.

"I could really use a hug right now," she whispered, looking at the figure on the shelf. "Daddy always knew when I needed one."

Krac didn't wait. He stepped forward and wrapped his arms around her. His eyes closed as she stiffened in resistance before tentatively wrapping her arms around his waist. The heat inside him turned into an inferno. For the first time in his life, he wanted someone for himself.

"I should not have said what I did," he admitted.

"No, you shouldn't have," she agreed as she rested her cheek against his chest and sighed. "Why did you?"

"Because I do not want you to think of that other male," he grunted.

Skeeter pulled back and tilted her head back. "Why?" She asked, confused.

"Because," Krac whispered. "Because I wanted to kiss you and I did not like that you might be thinking of him when I did."

Skeeter shook her head. "That will never happen," she murmured as he bent his head. "He didn't fire me up the way you do," she breathed as their lips touched.

Chapter 16

"What part of 'no' didn't you get? Do you not have any balls? I have to tell you, I do and I'd like to keep them," Froget's voice growled from the doorway.

Krac hissed when Skeeter bit down on his lower lip as she jumped at the sound of Froget's voice behind her. He released a deep, controlled breath as he pulled back. His eyes narrowed on the other male who was standing in the doorway to Skeeter's room with his hands on his hips and impatiently tapping one large foot.

"Sorry," Skeeter whispered, pulling back.

"You are not the one who needs to be sorry. I think I will kill him so he does not interrupt us again," Krac growled. "I have killed for much less."

"Fine! Threaten me all you want, but when you go to take a piss and have to sit down, think of me laughing at you from the great beyond," Froget snapped. "Now, get your ass out of her bedroom."

Skeeter's giggle wasn't the only one that echoed in the room. Three pairs of eyes turned to the bed. Violet was sitting up, the large red Triterian held tightly to her chest as she looked at them with sleepy eyes.

"Ohhhh, Frog said a bad word," she giggled. "Mommy says she is going to wash Uncle Rorrak's mouth out with soap when he does that. Skeeter, are you going to wash Frog's mouth out? Why was Uncle Krac kissing you like daddy kisses mommy? Is he your Prince Charming?"

Skeeter blushed furiously as she tucked a wayward strand of hair behind her ear. "I... He... Back to sleep, little one."

"I'm thirsty," Violet yawned.

"I'll get the kid a drink. Uncle Krac will help me to make sure I do it right, won't you Uncle Krac?" Frog replied as he looked pointedly at Krac's larger form.

Krac waited until he was in the corridor before he turned to Froget with a fierce scowl. "I don't like you very much."

"Well, that certainly has me shaking in my boots," Froget replied sarcastically, rolling his large eyes.

"It should," Krac growled as Froget started toward the galley.

The soft giggles coming from the bedroom let him know that both females had heard his remark and Froget's response. He shook his head. Back on Earth he was considered a monster. He was something created in a lab by scientists from horrible alien creatures from the past. Just the color of his skin was enough to send most men and all women except for Anastasia and Gracie screaming in terror. That was why he normally wore a cloak to conceal his identify.

The female in the other room had turned his carefully controlled, organized world upside down in a matter of hours. He glared at the back of the male walking away from him. His eyes narrowed as a slow, menacing smile curved his lips.

If that little amphibian piece of shit interrupts me when I'm kissing Skeeter again, I'm going to eject his green ass out the nearest disposal tube, Krac thought as he adjusted the front of his pants.

..*

The next four days were spent in a dance of frustration with Frog and Krac squaring off on either side of the Skeeter. It was so bad, even Violet was watching the two males with delight.

Frog had taken it upon himself to be Skeeter's chaperone and protector. If he wasn't with her, he made sure Violet was. Skeeter couldn't help but laugh when she got up the first morning and almost tripped over her co-pilot who had made a pallet on the floor outside of her and Violet's door.

"What are you doing sleeping on the floor?" She had exclaimed in surprise.

"Making sure that horny gray bastard isn't sleeping in your bed and you are not in his," Frog had replied grouchily.

"There isn't enough room in Skeeter's bed, silly," Violet giggled. "And she can't sleep in his bed because she has to sleep with me so I don't get scared."

"You just remember that," Frog had muttered before he grabbed his blanket and pillow and stomped off.

Now, she sighed in regret as she stared out the front viewport of the *Lulu Belle*. The *Conqueror* had contacted them to inform them that it would be within visual in two hours. If that wasn't bad enough, the *Raven* and the *Galaxy* would arrive shortly after.

That meant her time to discover if there could be something between her and Krac was about to end.

"What is wrong?" A deep voice asked from behind her.

Skeeter turned in the Captain's chair to see Krac standing in the doorway. She had never realized how small the bridge of the freighter was until he stepped inside it. Truthfully, there was just enough room around the Captain and co-pilot chairs to access some of the instrument panels but for her, he filled every part of it.

"I was just thinking," she replied, gazing at his dark features and thinking he looked sexier every day. "We've only got a couple more hours until your friends arrive. I'm going to cry when Violet leaves. It has been fun having her around. I'll miss her."

"Is she the only one you will miss?" Krac asked in a husky voice as he stepped closer to her chair. "Is she?"

Skeeter leaned back as he placed his hands on the arms of the chair, caging her in. She licked her lips as he leaned forward. Desire flared hot inside her, pooling low between her legs and making her ache.

"No," she whispered.

"Good," Krac muttered before sealing his lips hungrily over hers.

He was very close to killing her damn co-pilot. He didn't care that the male was just being protective of her. He didn't care that he had spent the last four days and nights trying to rationalize what was happening to him.

There was nothing rational about the hunger burning deep inside him. His cock was in a perpetual state of hardness. Even trying to shut down so he could rest did not work. He had never dreamed before, but the last two nights had been filled with brilliant images of a soft, curvy redhead. He woke covered in sweat and shaking. He did not understand what was happening and it confused and enraged him.

He swallowed the soft groan that escaped her as she responded to him. It pulled at something deep inside him. He slid his arms around her waist, lifting her until she was pressed against his hard length. He kissed her deeper, wanting, needing something that he couldn't put a name to. He hurt. He hurt in a way that no matter how hard he tried to turn off his nerve-endings, he still ached.

"What are you doing to me?" He asked roughly as he continued to press kisses along her jaw. "I hurt. I cannot get it to stop. I want… need…." His voice died and his eyes widened in shock when he felt a slender hand wrap around him.

"I need you too," Skeeter whispered as she wrapped her fingers around his cock and stroked the hard length. "Ohhh, you feel so good. Please tell me you ejected Frog out into space and Violet is sound asleep."

"Skeeter…," Krac's throat worked up and down in time with her hand. "Skeeter, I… what… this is…."

"I want to taste you," she muttered impatiently, pulling at the waist of his pants. "Where is Frog and Violet?"

"I... in the... galley," he wheezed as the front of his pants finally opened under her persistent assault. "What are you...? Oh hell...." He choked out.

* * *

Skeeter was on fire. She had never felt this wanton or desperate with Terry. This was completely different. Before she had been more curious than aroused. Now, now she was aching and throbbing and just plain desperate.

She sank back down into the Captain's chair, pulling Krac forward by his cock. Her eyes widened at the long, thick length trapped in her hand. The end was rounded and a slight drop of pearly crème was beaded at the top while the rest of his length throbbed in her palm.

Skeeter leaned forward and touched the tip of her tongue to the creamy drop. A combination of sweet and salty exploded over it. She barely heard his explanation of where Frog and Violet were. She hoped they stayed busy long enough for her to convince Krac that he wanted to stay with her for a few extra years or decades.

Decades were good, she thought as she slid her mouth over him.

"I... you... yessssss!" Krac's deep voice echoed in her ears. "Yessss, oh yes."

Each word fired Skeeter to explore him further. His hands rested lightly on her shoulders before curling in her hair almost as if he was afraid that she might stop.

There was no way that was going to happen. Her own body was pulsing with his. She parted her legs enough to press his knee closer to the chair so she could press her own slick clit against him in a desperate measure to relieve the pressure building inside her.

"Please," she whispered, pulling back just far enough to let him know what she needed. "Oh Krac, please. My shirt. Take it off. Please. I need to feel your hands on me."

* * *

Krac's throat worked up and down in silent awe. He swore his eyes crossed when she wrapped her hot mouth around him. He had heard the scientists and the guards joke about sex, but he had never had any desire to experience it. It would have been another way for them to control him.

The one time they tried, he had remained unresponsive. He had not felt any pleasure or need at the female's touch. The thought of that other female touching him the way Skeeter was would have been repulsive to him. Fortunately, once they realized that he wasn't interested they had dismissed that part of their research much to his relief.

Even in the six years of his freedom he had not been drawn to any female, well except for maybe Gracie. She was the only female besides Anastasia that didn't flinch when he walked into the room. Anastasia was... Anastasia. She was pleasing to look at but had never shown any physical interest in him; of course, neither had Gracie.

He had once kissed a barmaid. He did that as a cover to transfer the tracking device Altren Proctor's bodyguard had tried to plant on him. He had slipped it into the female's clothing. He had to wash his mouth out afterwards to dispel the awful taste of her.

This though, this was beyond anything he had ever been exposed to. The rush of feelings was playing havoc with his nervous system. His body was so sensitive he felt like every touch, every stroke of her hands and mouth was a direct assault on his nerve-endings.

"Please, I need you to touch me," Skeeter's voice echoed huskily in his ears.

"Your shirt," he muttered. "I... how do I remove it without destroying it?"

Skeeter's soft laugh sent a wave of heated breath over his cock. He moaned as it reacted to the heat, demanding he slide it back between her sweet lips. All he knew was if something wasn't done soon, some way to relieve the pressure building inside him, his cock and his balls, he was sure that he might just explode.

Stop it, he demanded, trying to command his cock to obey his control. Instead, it jerked up and down as if mocking him.

He watched in awe as Skeeter undid the buttons holding her shirt closed and slid her top free until it fell on the seat behind her. Her breasts were held up by a dark red, lacy contraption that looked painful to him. His fingers itched and moved on their own. He released his breath in a long sigh as they caressed the soft skin of her shoulders before moving further down.

He started shaking when she released the front of the lacy garment and it fell on top of her discarded shirt. She sat up straighter in the chair, pressing the hot seam between her legs against his knee while one slender hand reached up and drew his hand down over her lush breast.

His hand slid around the soft mound, lifting it even as his thumb and forefinger moved instinctively to capture the taut nipple. Her loud moan around his cock fired his blood. His hips began moving on their own, rocking faster and faster. The movement caused his knee to press harder into her. His breathing increased as her eyes rose to watch him as he gazed down at her.

The friction of her hand and mouth combined with the erotic sight was more than his mind and body could handle. His other hand reached down and captured her other breast, squeezing her tightly as the pressure built.

This was it. This is what he had been feeling the last few days, but only a thousand times worse. A pleasure that was almost painful. The deep burning in his loins, pooling in his balls that woke him up shaking and sweating.

He exploded when her other hand came up and cupped his taut sack, rolling it gently between her fingers as she sucked deeply on him. He let go of her breasts and grabbed the back of the chair so he wouldn't collapse as fireworks exploded through his shaking body.

"Ahhhh!" He cried out, his eyes closing as pleasure burst through his entire frame until he thought he would die from it. "Yessss."

Skeeter's soft whimpering grew louder as she continued to suck on him as she pressed frantically against his bent knee. A moment later, her loud moan drew a long hiss from him as her lips tightened around him.

They stayed frozen in the aftermath of their climaxes for several long moments before Skeeter slowly melted back into the chair, releasing his still throbbing cock. Krac shuddered as her lips slowly slid over the ultra-sensitive head of his cock. His head dropped forward and he opened his eyes to stare down into her flushed face.

Her eyes were closed and her soft, swollen lips were slightly parted and a bright pink. He fought to draw in a breath. A part of his mind was trying to process what just happened while his body was still reeling from it. This was beyond anything in his previous experience. His gaze ran over the delicate features before they hardened in determination. Whatever just happened had sealed Skeeter's fate. She was his now. He would never let her go and he would kill anyone who tried to take her from him.

He was about to inform her of his decision when the lights on the console began flashing and a small alarm echoed, startling them both. His face darkened at the sound. It was the *Lulu Belle's* security system that he had repaired. The freighter had been breached.

Chapter 17

"What's going on?" Skeeter asked as her eyes flew open to look up at him with dazed, unfocused eyes. She sat up in the chair, pulling her shirt and bra out from under her. She ignored the bra. Her hands were shaking too much to bother with it. Instead, she slid her shirt on and fumbled with the buttons, trying to close the front of it. "I didn't hit anything. Why are the alarms sounding?"

"It is your security system. There has been a breach," Krac growled in anger and frustration. "I need to connect to your computer system."

"I have a security system?" She asked in surprise, watching as he slid into the co-pilot's chair and pulled a small tablet lying on the console toward him. It lit up the moment he laid his palm over it. A moment later, the freighter's console lit up with information. "Oh, wow! I didn't know you could do that."

Krac turn his head so that Skeeter couldn't see the effect her words had on him. After what she had just done to him, shared with him, it hurt that she might reject him as she saw him for what he really was... a monster created in a lab.

He pushed his feelings aside, instead focusing on the information pouring in. There was a hull breach in the upper emergency access. He patched into his own starship, using the sensors on it to read the surrounding area. He swore silently when he detected the registration marks of Tillman's sleek starship.

"Skeeter, what in the....? Oh no, you did not," Froget stopped mid-sentence, staring at Skeeter's unevenly button top and the red, lacy bra in her hand. "Really? I leave you alone for twenty minutes and you two act like a couple of horny..."

"Frog!" Skeeter hissed with a warning glance at Violet before turning and redoing the buttons on her top. "Did you know we have a security system?"

"It works?" Froget asked in surprise before a scowl darkened his face. "What is going on?"

"There is a breach in the upper emergency access that connects to Cargo Bay 2," Krac replied in a monotone as he relayed the information coming in. "There are two males."

"Is it pirates?" Skeeter asked, pulling Violet protectively closer to her.

"No," Krac bit out sharply. "It is the men who attacked Kordon and Gracie and took Violet."

"Skeeter, I'm scared," Violet whispered, raising her arms up. "I don't like them. They hurt my daddy."

Skeeter reached down and picked Violet up in her arms, hugging her close. "It's okay, baby. We won't let them get you, will we Krac?"

Krac's eyes softened as he looked at the scared expression on both Skeeter and Violet's faces. The thought of anything happening to either one of them caused a deep rage to build inside him. It looked like he was about to be given an opportunity to learn more about what the New Order wanted from Gracie; but first, he needed to make sure Skeeter and Violet were tucked away somewhere safe.

"Frog, protect them with your life," Krac growled, standing up.

"Where do you think you are going? You said there are at least two men. Are you planning on taking them both out?" Frog asked, pulling the small knives he kept at his waist.

Krac looked down at the small male. "Keep them safe, Froget," he growled menacingly. "I will come for you next if you do not."

"Fine! Play the hero. Go have fun. I'll keep them safe. Besides," he added. "If they kill you it will save Ti'Death the hassle when he finds out what you did with Skeeter."

"Frog!" Skeeter exclaimed, mortified.

Krac's eyes narrowed as his mouth tightened into a grim line. "These are not space pirates, Froget. These are highly trained assassins with one goal and one goal only – to get to Gracie Jones-Jefe any way they can. The future of Earth depends on the outcome of this war. They will not hesitate to kill you and Skeeter to get to Violet."

Froget's expression turned serious and he nodded. "Go. I'll protect them. With my life, I swear."

Krac nodded before he glanced once more at Skeeter and strode from the bridge. He hadn't had time to fix all of the sensors for the PLT's. He would have to rely on the information the freighter could give him as they approached.

He slid his hand over one of the door panels to check which had been compromised. One of the things he had done when he tapped into the system on the bridge was to seal all doors. He would be able to tell where the men went by which doors opened.

A grim satisfaction coursed through him when he saw they were in the upper platform area of Cargo Bay 2. The freighter wasn't that large. The Trident Class IV was slightly over two hundred and twenty meters long with three levels. All but fifty meters was for cargo. The remaining fifty meters made up the living quarters. A normal crew between two and four was the standard for a freighter this size if fully operational. The two cargo bays were divided to handle different size cargo. The upper bay was for smaller shipments while the lower bay could handle up to two small transport shuttles.

Krac was already mapping out the area for possible locations for ambush, either by him or the assassins who had breached the ship. Each bay had several narrow maintenance storage areas and one larger room set aside for operating the motorized lifts that moved the cargo. He could override the system and use those as a distraction if necessary.

His mouth tightened as another door was overridden. This one on the lower level. They had split up. He had no idea which man was Harden. That was his primary target. He was likely the more dangerous of the two and would be the leader. He was the one that Krac needed to find if he wanted to get the information he wanted.

* * *

"Skeeter, I want you to take Violet back to your cabin and seal it," Froget ordered as he opened a small panel near the co-pilot's seat. Inside were several small but deadly laser pistols. "Don't open it for anyone except Krac or me."

"Can't we just seal them in the cargo bays and wait for help?" Skeeter asked, holding Violet in a fierce hug. "I mean, the Zion warships are only about an hour or so away. Surely we can lock them out and wait for more help."

Froget paused as he checked the charges on each of the three pistols that he had stored in case of a breach. He glanced up into Skeeter's frightened face. She was very pale and her eyes were wide with fear.

"I don't think these men will let a few sealed doors stop them, Skeeter," Froget reluctantly admitted. "Go on. Go seal yourself in the cabin. Krac and I will hold them off long enough for more help to come."

"Frog," Skeeter whispered as tears threatened to blind her. "I… please be careful."

"Here, take this, but be careful. It's fully charged and set to kill. Don't press the trigger unless you know who and what you are aiming at," he warned.

Skeeter reached out her left hand and took the laser pistol with a nod. She didn't tell him that she knew how to fire one. Bulldog had insisted that she be a superior marksman before he let her go off on her own. It hadn't taken much insisting. She didn't know if she had it in her to kill someone, but she did know that if push came to shove, she wouldn't go down without a fight.

"I won't," she replied before turning and hurrying down the corridor toward her cabin.

"Skeeter," Violet whimpered.

"What, baby?" She whispered as she stepped into her cabin.

"I wish my mommy and daddy were here," Violet sniffed, burying her head in Skeeter's neck.

"Me too, sweetheart. I wish my daddy was here as well," Skeeter murmured, setting the lock on the door. "How about we play a game?"

"What kind of game?" Violet asked, pulling back to look up.

"Hide and seek. Let's see if we can find some good hiding places in here so if the bad men come in, they won't find you," Skeeter said with a shaky smile. "I bet we can find some really good places where you could hide."

Violet nodded solemnly before her eyes turned to look at the bed where the stuffed Triterian was tucked in under the covers. She reached out her hand for it. Skeeter smiled as she picked up the little stuffed creature that Tila had made her when she was little.

Tila had known how scared Skeeter was to sleep alone and had made the stuffed creature in the image of Bulldog. Skeeter still remembered the story that Tila told her when she gave it to her the first night she slept in her own room.

"This is a magical Triterian," Skeeter whispered as she handed it to Violet. "Just like my daddy. Whenever you get scared or danger comes near, hold it tight, close your eyes and it will come alive and protect you. Nothing can defeat it, for it is a mighty Razor-tooth Triterian, the fiercest creature in all the star systems."

"Like the magic dragon that protected you when your real mommy and daddy died?" Violet asked, looking at Skeeter with her big green eyes.

"Just like that. I closed my eyes and wished for the fiercest dragon in all the world to come protect me and my daddy appeared. I knew the moment I saw him he could keep the bad men from ever getting me," Skeeter said, sitting on the edge of her bed.

"Just like Uncle Krac? He won't let the men get us. He is big and strong like a dragon," Violet whispered. "Daddy says he is a… is a… an ass."

Skeeter's lips twitched at Violet's description. "I'm sure he is at times," she chuckled as she pulled Violet close and pressed a kiss to her forehead.

He is a very lovable one, too, she couldn't help thinking as she closed her eyes and prayed that he would be kept safe.

* * *

"You go low," Harden said. "Find the gray bastard and kill him. I'll find the girl and anyone else and take them out."

"What about Crane?" Moss asked.

"He will find the kid. He had to secure the ship. We have twenty minutes to get in and out if we don't want to fight the damn Zion military," Harden growled. "I want to be out of here before they arrive."

Moss nodded and turned. He ran down the long platform, letting his eyes sweep the upper cargo bay.

Once he reached the end, he grabbed the thick metal handholds on each side and slid down the ladder, ignoring the individual rings. He was focused on one thing and one thing only, kill the male who had killed his brother.

Harden briefly watched Moss before dismissing the other male. He didn't expect him to survive. He knew what the Alluthan hybrids could do. He had watched one of the bastards in action. What was left behind was not a pretty picture.

Chapter 18

Krac moved through the lower cargo bay, pausing behind one of the few containers in it. He let his eyes sweep the area. He pulled on his other senses to help him locate the male he knew was in here. A slight sound to his left had him turning in the opposite direction to go around the tall structures.

"I know you are here," the male's voice called out. "Fight me. One on one."

Krac's eyes narrowed at the challenge. He had expected the male to try to ambush him, not outright call him out. He glanced around the side of the container and watched as the male stepped out into the open area.

He recognized the huge male as being one of the men from the medical tower, the one who had grabbed Violet. He had also grabbed the wounded man. Krac ran a comparison of the two men in his mind. The similarities between their eyes, nose, mouths and bone structure suggested a close DNA relationship existed between the two.

"I will kill you," Krac stated calmly as he stepped out. "Like I did the male."

"You killed Mace. He was my brother. Now, I will kill you," Moss replied angrily.

"Why is the New Order after Gracie?" Krac asked, stepping lightly to the side as the male shifted.

"I don't know," Moss said. "I don't care. You killed Mace. That is all I care about."

Krac felt a moment of regret that the huge male was going to die. It was obvious he was not very intelligent. His brother had probably used his larger strength to his advantage. Unfortunately, that would not change the male's fate. He needed to eliminate him before Harden found Skeeter and Violet.

"Where is the other male?" Krac asked, shifting again as the other male did.

"He is going to kill the girl. He's mad she stole the kid." Moss shrugged. "She shouldn't have made him mad. He is mean when he is mad."

Krac became still. "So am I," he replied before he struck.

He caught the male in the side, but the blow was deflected as the male twisted in a surprisingly fast move. He ignored the blow to his own back as he turned. They faced off, slowly circling each other. Krac ignored the sharp pain of the knife wound to his back. He had already sent the command for the nanobots in his bloodstream to repair the damage to his kidney which had been pierced by the long, sharp blade.

He jerked back when the male swung out his hand with the knife. His own hand came down and gripped the thick wrist and twisted it sharply. The male was prepared and rolled with movement, pulling out of his grasp. That move prevented Krac from snapping the large male's wrist.

"You are strong," Moss commented as he surged to his feet. "I'm strong too. You cannot beat me."

"I have no desire to beat you," Krac replied, shifting to his left as another swipe aimed at his throat this time swept by him. "I aim to kill you."

Moss grinned. "Then we are the same."

Krac moved, stepping into the male this time as he struck. He shut down the pain sensors inside his body as the knife went deep between his ribs. Instead, he focused on wrapping his hands on each side of the male's head and twisting. The move pulled the knife across, opening up a three inch slice along his ribcage, but it gave him the best advantage at ending the fight as quickly as possible. With a quick, hard jerk he snapped the male's neck.

"No," Krac muttered as he released the male, letting him drop to the floor of the cargo bay. "We are not."

He grimaced as he pulled the knife out of his body. He stumbled a little as he turned and braced his right hand against one of the cargo containers. Drawing in a deep breath, he focused on healing the damage. A soft curse escaped as it took a little longer than he liked to heal. He needed to get to an access panel so he could see where the other male had gone.

Pushing away from the container, he focused on the lower exit. He was almost to it when a sharp blow to the center of his back threw him forward. He cursed that he hadn't checked the area more thoroughly as darkness descended around him. His last conscious thought was to activate the nanobots to repair the damage as quickly as possible, even as his body shut down to prevent excessive blood loss.

* * *

"Where's the female and the kid?" Harden asked darkly.

Froget clutched his side where a laser shot had pierced him. The male had surprised him when he dropped down out of the conduit tubes running along the ceiling. He was able to get a few hits of his own as he watched in satisfaction at the blood running down the human's face before the male had shot him.

"Safe," Froget growled back in defiance. "You're a dead man. There are three Zion warships headed this way. You'll never get the kid before they get here."

"Wrong answer, little man," Harden replied as he fired another shot into Froget's thigh. He watched in satisfaction as the creature howled in pain as he collapsed. "Now, let's try this again. I ask you a question. You answer it truthfully. If you don't, I fire another shot into you until you tell me what I want."

"You'll... you are going to kill me anyway," Froget hissed hoarsely. "Why should I tell you anything?"

Harden shook his head. It was always the same. The last act of defiance, the hope that something would save the poor fool before they begged for their life. Unfortunately, he didn't have time to enjoy disillusioning the little green creature. The male was right. If he didn't get what he wanted in the next few minutes, he would either be a dead man or leave empty handed. Neither choice was in his plans.

Pulling out a sharp laser knife, he knelt over the fallen body and drove it into the wound in the amphibian's leg. A loud tortured scream filled the corridor as he twisted it. His other hand pressed down on the male's shoulder to hold him still.

"Where is the girl and the kid?" Harden asked one last time.

"Go to hell," Froget panted.

Harden shook his head as he pulled the knife out of the wound. He looked down at the pale figure trapped under him. Always the same, stupid heroics all for nothing.

"You can wait for me there," Harden replied as he drove the knife in his hand through the creature's heart.

"NO!!!!!" A hoarse cry echoed behind him. "Frog!"

Harden's lips curved as he slowly rose and turned. He had hoped the screams from the creature would draw out his prey. He figured if the female was compassionate enough to steal the kid, she would have some feelings for a member of her crew.

So predictable, he thought as he stared at the pale, shaking figure standing outside of one of the crew cabins.

His eyes flashed over the curvy redhead holding a small laser pistol aimed at his chest. It wouldn't do her any good. She could shoot him all she wanted. He had paid a small fortune for the special material that made up his clothing. It could absorb the blasts from any small to medium size laser pistol or laser sword rendering them useless. The only place that was vulnerable was his head. Very few adversaries went for the head shot first. That gave him the advantage of killing them before they recognized their mistake. He didn't have to worry about that with the terrified female standing between him and his prize.

"Where's the kid?" He asked, taking a step away from the dead male. He palmed the knife at his waist as he moved forward. "Tell me and I might not make you scream as loud as your friend there did."

* * *

Skeeter refused to look at Frog's lifeless body. She couldn't. Instead, her eyes stared into the cold eyes of the human male. He was the one from the Part's shop on Pryus. She refused to look anywhere but at his eyes. Bulldog said a person's eyes told you about their soul. He said if they were cold and lifeless, so was the person. She had once asked him what he saw when he looked into her eyes. He had told her he saw the beauty of the universe.

She blinked rapidly when she thought of Frog's big, round eyes. They had always been filled with warmth, humor and a touch of exasperation when he looked at her. Tears filled her eyes at the thought of never seeing that look again.

"Why?" She choked out. "Why did you have to... to... kill him? He never hurt anybody. He..." Her voice broke as the reality of what was happening sunk in. "He was my friend."

"My heart is truly bleeding," Harden replied sarcastically. "Where's the kid?"

Skeeter shook her head and took a step backwards as he continued toward her. "Stop. You can't have her. She's just a little girl. Leave her alone."

"Can't do that, sweetheart. It's a shame you have to die. I'm sure we could have had a good time otherwise, but I just don't have the time to be nice to you. I need the kid now," Harden snapped, stopping when Skeeter widened her stance and aimed the pistol.

"No," she whispered.

"Wrong answer, sweetcake. Just like your friend. Bulldog should have taught you never to take something that isn't yours. You might have lived if he had," Harden said in a sharp voice at the same time as he flicked his wrist.

Skeeter jerked and tilted, but his words kept her focused long enough to pull the trigger. She remembered one very important piece of advice Bulldog gave her when he was training her to shoot. A piece of advice Harden obviously wasn't expecting from the stunned look on his face.

If you have to shoot someone, Lulu Belle, Bulldog's voice whispered in her mind as a small hole appeared between Harden's eyes, *make sure it is between the eyes. A head shot will stop just about anything.*

Her eyes fluttered as blood began to trickle from it. She barely heard the hoarse curse as her body fell in sync with the other male. She hoped Violet was right when she said nothing could stop her Uncle Krac because he was now the only thing standing between the bad guys and her.

Crane stood frozen, staring in disbelief at the corridor of bodies. He jumped when a small warning signal buzzed at his waist. He glanced down at Harden's unseeing eyes with another curse.

Turning on his heel, he rushed back the way he had come. As far as he was concerned, this mission was over. There was no way he was about to take on three Zion warships. He was just glad that he didn't have to face the big gray bastard that had taken Moss out. He had watched the fight between the two males, waiting for a clear shot from the upper platform with the laser rifle he carried. It had been a lucky break when the male had turned his back, giving him a clear shot.

It is time to disappear, Crane thought as he climbed into the pilot's seat of the sleek starship that Tillman had loaned them. *If Tillman doesn't kill me, the Leader will. Thank God those Zion bastards aren't going to give a damn about a couple of short haul freighter crew or a lab rat as long as they get the kid back or I'd really be in deep shit.*

Chapter 19

Krac's mind came back online before the rest of his body. He quickly ran an internal scan. Flexing his shoulders, he felt a small twinge of pain, but it quickly subsided. He pushed up off the cold metal floor of the cargo bay. Either Harden had circled around or there had been another, uncounted for, intruder.

He rose to his feet. Crossing to the panel by the door, he slapped his hand and connected to the security system. His lips tightened when he saw that a clear path to the upper living levels and the bridge were open. As a last thought, he searched out the door to Skeeter's cabin. It had been sealed earlier. Dread pooled low in his stomach when the computer showed it was open.

Ignoring the still healing wounds in his side and back, he broke into a run. He breathed evenly in and out as he focused on the layout of the freighter, hoping Frog had found a safe place for Skeeter and Violet to hide. He connected to the comlink in his ear.

"Froget, status," he ordered as he rounded the corner near the galley. "Froget, give me a status now!"

His breathing began to grow erratic when he didn't receive an answer. He cursed when he realized Skeeter must not be wearing one or she would have answered him. He rounded the last corner leading to Skeeter's cabin and the bridge. Bile choked him when he saw Froget's blank stare and the blood pooled around his body.

His eyes moved over the body of another male. This one he recognized immediately as the assassin called Harden. A thin stream of congealing blood ran from the center of his forehead down to his hairline.

"No," he whispered stumbling over Harden's outstretched arm when he saw Skeeter's still body lying outside her cabin door. "Please, no. Please, please, no."

He stumbled forward and fell to his knees next to Skeeter's pale face. He didn't know who he was begging for mercy. He just knew he would never survive the pain that was threatening to overwhelm him if she was dead. His fingers shook as he gently caressed her pale cheek before his hand moved down to the knife protruding from her chest.

"Krac!"

His head jerked up at the sound of his name. Bran and Cooraan stood poised to fight while several other Zion warriors checked the bodies of the other two males. Desperation surged through him at the look of compassion and regret on their faces.

The hand laying on Skeeter's chest moved ever so slightly. He could feel the rise and fall as she breathed. She was still alive.

"Please. Help her," he croaked out. "She is alive."

Bran cursed, stepping forward to kneel next to the female as he snapped out an order for a medical team. "Where is Violet Jefe?"

Krac's eyes moved to the dead assassin. There had been another intruder. The one that had shot him. Was it possible the male had escaped with Violet?

"I don't know. Froget and Skeeter were protecting her," he replied, looking back down at Skeeter's pale face.

"Let me take a look at her," a feminine voice murmured. "I need a stabilizer kit, stat!"

Krac stood up and took a reluctant step back when another member of Bran's crew passed him. He recognized the female as the Chief Medical Officer. He watched as she placed several stabilizer electrodes on Skeeter.

"Spread out!" Cooraan ordered the warriors. "Find Violet Jefe and search for anyone else that might be on board the freighter."

"Krac," a very faint voice whispered.

Krac took a step forward as the medic moved to the side. He knelt down next to Skeeter as her eyes fluttered as she regained consciousness. He tenderly lifted her hand when she struggled to reach out for him.

"Shush," he murmured. He ignored those standing around him, watching in disbelief as he tenderly caressed her. "You will get better."

A faint smile pulled at her lips at his growled order before it died. "Frog," she whispered as tears filled her eyes and overflowed. "He... killed Frog."

"I know," Krac said gently.

"Ask her where Violet is," Bran ordered from behind him.

"You'd better hurry if you have any questions for her," Toolas warned, looking at the tablet in her hand.

"Her blood pressure is dropping. I need to get her back to the *Conqueror* if you want me to save her."

Krac's eyes flashed in anger as he felt Skeeter's hand tremble violently in his. He briefly closed his eyes and breathed deeply before opening them, knowing Bran was right. They needed to know about Violet. The longer it took, the more danger she could be in. He nodded before focusing down on Skeeter's pale face.

"Skeeter, where is Violet? Was she taken?" He asked, leaning closer when her lips barely moved to answer him.

He sat back and nodded to Toolas as Skeeter's hand went limp in his. He heard Toolas call out urgently to the medics to get Skeeter back to the *Conqueror* stat. He rose and moved to the side as they carefully lifted her onto the stretcher. He stood frozen against the wall, pain radiating through him. It felt as if his heart was being ripped out of his body as he watched the small group hurry away.

"Krac. Krac, what did she say?" Bran asked impatiently.

"Magic words," he murmured, finally turning to look at the Zion Grand Admiral. "We will find Violet if we say the magic words."

Cooraan looked back and forth between Krac and Bran before shaking his head. "Does anyone know what in the hell that means?"

Krac looked back at Cooraan before he turned to gaze at the twinkling lights in Skeeter's cabin. He wouldn't allow Violet to see Froget's body. He remembered the haunted look in Skeeter's eyes when she told him about what happened to her when her parents were killed. He would not let that happen to Gracie and Kordon's daughter.

"I know," Krac replied quietly. "Clear out the bodies. The amphibian male is to be treated as a warrior. He deserves a warrior's death rite. I will examine the other body and dispose of it later."

"What of Kordon and Gracie's daughter?" Cooraan asked in frustration.

Krac turned and looked at both men with a calm determination. "I will not let her see this. The green male was a friend to her. I will not let her see him like this. Ty and Malik will be here any moment. She knows both of them. I will release her to them once they arrive. Until then, I will stay with her."

Krac didn't give either male a chance to argue. He stepped into Skeeter's cabin and palmed the door control, closing it and sealing him and Violet in the magical world that Skeeter had created.

His eyes swept the area. It seemed impossible that there could be any place for Violet to hide in the small room but he knew she was there. He could feel it.

"Ally, ally in come free," he called out quietly. "Violet, it is… Uncle Krac. You are safe, little one."

A panel on the wall behind the small table pushed open. Krac's expression softened when a faint light peeked out of the narrow gap as it opened further. He crossed the room and moved the chair that was in front of the panel.

Kneeling on one knee, he pulled the panel the rest of the way off. Inside was a large enough area for a small adult to hide inside. Skeeter had placed a thick blanket on the cold metal floor of the compartment to pad it. Violet knelt on the blanket, surrounded by the stuffed creatures that normally littered Skeeter's bed. Her thin arms were wrapped tightly around the dark red Triterian. A small emergency torch was set up in the corner and lit the inside with a soft glow.

"Hi," Violet said, looking at Krac with eyes far older than they should. "Where's Skeeter?"

Krac's throat worked up and down as he saw the sadness and fear in the crystal clear green depths. He held his arms out and waited until Violet was safely in them before rising. He turned and crossed back over to the bed and sat down, settling Violet on his lap as he tried to think of how much he should tell her.

"Is she with her mommy and daddy now?" Violet asked quietly, looking down at the stuffed Triterian in her arms. "She said if she didn't come and get me not to worry. She said… she might have to go see her mommy and daddy and I shouldn't be sad if she did."

Unfamiliar dampness blinded Krac at the soft words. His arms tightened around the tiny body in his arms and he wished desperately for the ice that had protected his heart to come back because the pain he was feeling right now was overwhelming his nervous system. He cleared his throat so he could answer Violet's softly spoken question.

"No," he responded hoarsely. "No, she is not with her mommy and daddy. She is being cared for. She... was hurt."

Violet sat quietly on his lap before she picked up his left hand in hers. She pushed at his fingers to let him know she wanted him to open them. When he did, she carefully laid the small sculpture that Skeeter had also given her in his palm.

"Skeeter gave this to me," Violet whispered. "She said you are like her daddy and it would keep me safe. I think she needs it more than me."

Krac looked at the small sculpture of Bulldog and swallowed. He remembered Skeeter's words as she tenderly held the small figurine of her 'father'.

"Most people think of him as a monster," Skeeter had softly reflected.

"But you didn't?" He remembered asking her quietly.

Her tender smile had spoken as much as her words had. *"No, never. While others saw his scary teeth and sharp claws, I saw my own personal dragon come to save and protect me. He was larger than life and the most beautiful creature I had ever seen. He still is. He's my hero and he always will be."*

His hand tightened around the figurine and he looked up at the twinkling lights as the impact of her meaning swept through him. A shudder shook his body as he fought to keep from roaring out his pain.

A knock on the door sounded to let him know that it was safe to leave the cabin. He rose stiffly with Violet quietly tucked in his arms. He carefully slipped the figurine into the pocket of his pants before palming the door open. Ty and Malik Jefe stood outside the door, waiting. They nodded to him even as they smiled at Violet, who smiled back at them.

"Hey little britches," Ty said affectionately. "Are you ready to go see your mommy and daddy?"

Krac handed Violet over when she reached for her uncle. He frowned when she turned in Ty's arms and held out the stuffed Triterian. He reached out automatically, taking it as she let go.

"This is Skeeter's," Violet said with a smile. "She likes to sleep with it. She says it keeps the bad dreams away."

Krac nodded tightly as he held it to his chest. He ignored the confused and amused glances from Ty and Malik as he did. It was a part of Skeeter.

He knew he should find out where Bran had taken Harden and the other male's bodies so he could see if there was anything he could use to identify the last intruder. He knew he should contact Roarrk and Anastasia to get an update on their end. He had already given the information about Tillman's personal starship to Roarrk. There was a hundred and one other things he knew he should be doing, but there was only one thing he was going to do.

"I will be on the *Conqueror* if you need me," Krac stated as he turned away. "Tell Kordon the next time there is a known threat to his family to have the damn healer come to his compound. I will not be saving his ass again."

Ty chuckled when Violet's face screwed up and her lips form an 'O'. "I know, little britches," Ty laughed. "Your mommy is going to find a bar of soap."

Malik turned to his brother with a frown. "What the hell just happened? I swear he was acting almost human!"

"Ohhhh, Uncle Malik said a bad word," Violet giggled before she yawned and laid her curly head on Ty's shoulder. "I want my mommy."

Ty rubbed Violet's back affectionately as he started after Krac. "Your mommy wants you too, little britches. We'll have you home safe and sound in no time."

Chapter 20

Krac sat next to the bed reading the information Roarrk had sent him. Every few minutes his eyes would wander over the still, pale figure quietly sleeping. He nodded when Toolas came in and walked over to the bed. He watched as the healer checked the monitor hooked up to Skeeter. He already knew what it said as he had tapped into it and received minute by minute updates.

He ignored the amused smile on Toolas' face as she noted the stuffed Triterian carefully tucked under the covers next to Skeeter, one of her slender arms carefully wrapped around it. Instead, he focused on the changes as she adjusted the medication. He noted that she had shut off the medication that was keeping Skeeter in a deep sleep.

"She is well enough to wake?" He asked.

Toolas glanced in surprise at the strange male who had been a constant presence in her medical unit for the past three days. Her eyes moved to where his fingers were entwined with the pale hand of the female. While a part of her itched to study the unusual male, another part understood that desire could be her last if she were to pursue it.

"Yes, she is well enough. She will be a little tender for a few days in the shoulder and chest area. If she takes it easy, she will be fine. The tissue regrowth is almost complete and there is no indication of leakage or additional blood loss where the wound was sealed. A few days of rest and she should be back to normal," Toolas assured him. "I'll inform the Grand Admiral that she should be well enough to transfer back to her freighter by tomorrow. I understand she lost her co-pilot. I'm sure the Grand Admiral will assign a warrior to help her return to the nearest Spaceport given what she has done for Councilman Jefe and his family."

"I will go with her," Krac said dismissively.

"Very well," Toolas replied. "I need to file my report. Is there anything else you need?"

"No," Krac said, shaking his head.

"I... very well," Toolas replied with a sigh of regret.

Krac nodded again. He could feel the curiosity pulling at the healer. He could see it in her eyes. He was used to it when he was around others, especially those who studied medicine. He knew she wanted to ask him questions and study him, but he'd had enough of that in his life.

He turned in his seat to stare down at the slender fingers in his hand. Now, he wanted more. For the past three days, he had thought long and hard about what he wanted. Before, he merely existed. First as a laboratory experiment then as a protector to the descendants of the Freedom Five. Never before had he thought of his own needs and desires. That had changed since he met Skeeter.

A ghost of a smile curled his lips as he remembered the first time he saw her standing in the corridor growling and clawing to get at Violet. He recalled his amazement when her slender arm came out of the sleeve of what he now knew was one of many strange articles of clothing that she liked to collect.

He chuckled softly as he remembered his shock when the head of the creature rolled across the floor. He realized now he was doomed the minute Skeeter's brilliant blue eyes connected with his. Sadness, a very unfamiliar feeling before he met Skeeter, tugged at him as he remembered Froget's demands to either kill them or help him get her to her cabin after she fainted at the sight of his blood.

He bowed his head as he remembered the funeral rite the Zion warriors had given the little amphibian male. Froget had received a full salute from the crews in honor of his sacrifice to protect the daughter of their former Grand Admiral and his human mate.

He looked up when the slender fingers in his hand tightened slightly. The blue eyes that he had fallen in love with stared back at him. Tears shimmered in the dim light as she gazed at him with a silent plea for comfort. He rose from the chair and slid his arms around her, pulling her close.

"It will be alright," he murmured as her body shook with her sobs. "I will protect you. I swear, Skeeter."

"Poor Frog," she whispered in a broken, husky whisper.

"He was a true warrior," Krac replied, rocking her back and forth in an attempt to comfort her. "He was given a warrior's funeral."

Krac didn't know what else to say or do. He just knew that each quiet sob, each tear she shed, tore at his heart. This, he realized, is what it meant to feel. This is what it meant to… love someone. He could feel her pain and grief as if it were his own.

After several minutes, he felt the fragile body in his arms began to wilt as exhaustion from her injuries and her tears pulled at her. He gently laid her back against the covers, soothingly brushing her hair away from her face. His thumb gently wiped at the stray tears that continued to fall even as her eyelids began to droop.

"Krac," her soft voice echoed in the quiet room.

"What, my beautiful red bird?" He whispered.

Her eyelashes fluttered open and she looked at him with a solemn expression. "Can I keep you for a few decades, maybe more?"

A smile tugged at his lips as he leaned forward to brush a light kiss across her forehead. "Maybe more," he answered near her ear. "I think I am in love with you, Lulu Belle Mann," he admitted before he pulled away.

A beautiful smile curved her pink lips even as her eyelashes lay like delicate crescents against her tear-stained cheeks. He continued to brush one hand soothingly over her hair. His other was entwined with hers. Her breathing evened out after several minutes and he knew she had fallen back asleep. He gently tucked the stuffed Triterian protectively against her before slipping his fingers from hers with regret. He nodded to Toolas who had been observing them. Instead of feeling resentful, he nodded his appreciation for her care and concern for his female.

She is mine, he thought as he answered the silent call coming in.

* * *

Krac stepped into the conference room off the bridge and nodded to the group of men sitting around it. Ty Jefe had taken his warship, *The Raven*, and was returning Violet to Kordon and Gracie. He moved closer to the windows, unable to sit as restless energy flowed through him. The attack on the *Lulu Belle* had brought the war closer to home. Before he had fought out of a sense of duty and loyalty to Anastasia. Now, he fought for personal reasons.

His eyes flickered to the split screens. One showed Anastasia with Roarrk standing behind her looking very grim. The other was Kordon Jefe.

"Toolas said Captain Mann will be well enough to transfer back to her freighter tomorrow. Once she has, we'll be heading back to Pryus. Tillman's starship has docked with it. Only one member of the crew disembarked," Bran stated, his eyes following as Krac moved into the shadows near the viewport.

"Tillman states his starship was stolen when it was docked for repairs six months ago. He has offered a substantial reward for its return. Personally, I think he is full of shit," Anastasia commented, sitting back in her chair only to jerk forward when Roarrk placed his hands on her shoulders. "He didn't report the theft until three weeks ago."

"What was his excuse?" Kordon asked calmly.

"He said he was not informed until then by his flight chief. He claims he has documentation to support his claims if I have any doubt," Anastasia replied sarcastically. "All doctored I'm sure."

"Krac, have you found anything from the men that were killed?" Kordon asked. "Also, Gracie and I would like to thank you for returning Violet to us. It is a debt we will never be able to repay."

Krac shuttered his eyes when all eyes turned to him. He refused to show how uncomfortable he was being the center of attention. He was used to being in the shadows.

"Your debt is not to me, but to Captain Mann. She is the one who rescued Violet from the assassins. Violet is well since her return?" Krac corrected.

The corner of Kordon's mouth curled upward and he nodded. "Oh yes. She has decided she is going to be a freighter captain now when she grows up," he said dryly. "She wants a pink one."

Chuckles echoed around the room at Kordon's statement. Krac's eyes flickered to the viewport where he could see the *Lulu Belle* off the port side. The lights from both the freighter and the *Conqueror* reflected off the outer hull highlighting the color. His eyes moved down the long surface toward the back where the shadowed outline of a dark red bird in flight was painted over the welded area that had been repaired.

"I learned very little from the men that I didn't already know," he replied, turning back to look at Kordon. "Harden Gimbal was an assassin for hire. He spent much of his youth in one of Earth's youth detention rehabilitation facilities before he vanished at the age of fourteen. He was wanted in at least three star systems for the murder of prominent members within their legal or political system. He was hired by Tillman's company four years ago to oversee the transport of defense equipment to some of the mining operations along the outer rim. One interesting pattern that I noticed was each of the mining facilities he delivered to were the ones attacked by the Alluthans."

Curses echoed throughout the room at Krac's last statement. He frowned as a new theory occurred to him. His eyes narrowed on Kordon as he ran the data he had stored on Harden, Tillman, the attacks on the Freedom Five descendants and the recent sudden interest in Gracie. That was one connection that none of them had connected until now.

"They want Gracie because of her knowledge of the Alluthans. She has been on board an Alluthan Mothership and lived. She knows their language, their computer systems and has firsthand knowledge of them both past and present," Krac murmured out loud.

Kordon's loud curse broke him out of his reverie. "Why? Why would they want to know about the Alluthans? The Mothership was destroyed!"

"One," Krac replied. "One Mothership. What happened to the debris from it?"

"We salvaged as much as we could," Bran said.

"The Zion military?" Krac asked with an intense stare.

"No," Cooraan interrupted. "The council hired a salvage company. Everything that was collected was delivered to Paulus for the Confederation's scientists to analyze."

"What company was hired?" Krac asked, already knowing the answer but wanting confirmation of his suspicions.

"Multi-Works," Anastasia hissed in dismay. "It is one of Tillman's subsidiaries."

"Anastasia, do you think Tillman could be the Leader of the New Order?" Kordon asked point blank.

"If he is, I would have already taken him out," Roarrk spoke up from behind Anastasia. "He's not, but he is working for the Leader."

"Are you sure? Everything is pointing to him?" Kordon insisted.

"He's a ruthless bastard, but he is a follower," Anastasia said. "I've had him followed for the past year. He was on Sallas when an attack on one of the council members was done. This one by the Leader himself."

"Which member? How can they be sure that it was the Leader?" Bran asked.

"It was my younger sister Morgan," Anastasia responded quietly. "She was in the wrong place at the wrong time."

"Couldn't she identify him?" Kordon demanded.

"No," Krac answered when Anastasia turned her head away to hide her grief. "Morgan was barely alive. She whispered that it was the Leader who attacked her before she lost consciousness."

"What did she tell you when she woke?" Kordon asked impatiently.

"She was in a coma for over a month. When she finally woke, she could remember nothing of the attack," Anastasia answered. "She has tried, but she remembers nothing."

Kordon sat back with a growl of frustration. "Then we are no closer to finding out what is going on than we were before," he retorted in a cold voice.

"What of Gracie? Has there been any more attacks?" Roarrk asked in concern. "If they want information about the Alluthans from her, they will try again."

"Two nights back an assault team tried to enter the compound," Kordon admitted. "We were aware of their arrival and were prepared. I've since moved with Gracie, Adam and Violet to a more secured location. Krac, we need to know why they want information on the Alluthans. There is something we are missing. This is beyond just the Earth council. I will bring it up with the Confederation Council members."

"I will get the information," Krac promised.

"Roarrk, you and Anastasia make sure you know every move that Tillman is making. Bran, make sure that every scrap of the Alluthan Mothership is accounted for. I will work with Gracie to see if there is anything that she might remember that can help. I want a report the moment you discover anything."

Krac listened as Kordon went over a few other items but they had little to do with him. Already, his mind was back on the brave and beautiful human female lying in the medical unit. He was torn between his duty to protect the Earth council and his need to protect Skeeter from additional harm.

There was only one person he trusted to protect her the way he would. One person in the universe who was as deadly as he was. It was time that he introduced himself to Skeeter's illustrious father – Bulldog Ti'Death.

Chapter 21

The next morning, Skeeter sat in the chair in the medical unit waiting for Krac. She had woken up feeling much better physically. Emotionally, she was still a wreck. Toolas told her that she was being given the all clear to return to the *Lulu Belle*. Every time she thought about the freighter, she thought about Frog and her eyes would fill with tears.

Poor Toolas had sat with her for nearly an hour and talked with her about her grief, explaining that it was natural and healthy to cry for someone she cared about. She had listened carefully to what the healer was saying. Even though she had dealt with her parents dying, she had been very young. This was really the first time that someone she had really cared about since she was grown had died. The fact that Frog died protecting her and Violet only made the pain ten-times worse. Toolas explained she might be feeling something called 'survivor's guilt'.

"It is perfectly natural, but you have to understand, your friend would not want you to remember him with sadness. Focus on the good times you had with him. It will help if you celebrate the time you spent with him," Toolas said gently.

"Can't you make her sadness go away?" Krac demanded, glaring at Toolas after he returned from his meeting. "You have medication. It takes away pain."

"Medication is merely a band aid," Toolas replied in exasperation. "What Skeeter is feeling will lessen with time. Eventually, she will be able to think of her friend without tears but with a smile. Skeeter, can you remember a special time with your friend?"

"Well, there was the time I backed into the pirate ship," Skeeter said with a small, shaky smile. "He was hopping up and down so much when the alarms went off that I thought he was going to hit his head on the ceiling." She gave a watery chuckle. "He could hop really, really high when he was mad."

Toolas laughed and nodded her head. "That is what I am talking about. Remember the good times."

Krac scowled at Toolas. "Almost getting hijacked by pirates is not something to laugh at," he retorted as he thought of what could have happened to Skeeter if the pirates had boarded the freighter.

Toolas crossed her arms and stared in exasperation at Krac. "That is not the point," she replied with a shake of her head.

"He... he... was always trying to get me to pay more attention to the controls," Skeeter whispered, her eyes filling with tears again. "I... should have... listened to him better."

Krac bent down and pulled Skeeter into his arms when she started sobbing again. He looked accusingly at Toolas and narrowed his eyes in warning. He was shocked when the healer just shook her head again and stood up.

"Where are you going?" Krac demanded as Toolas walked across the room toward her office. "Her eyes are still leaking."

"Yes, they are and they will continue to 'leak'. It is natural for most species to cry when they are sad or upset. Humans are especially susceptible to it," Toolas replied.

"But, how can I make her stop?" Krac asked desperately when he realized that the healer really was going to leave.

"Give her something else to think about," Toolas suggested with a raised eyebrow. "Something... more pleasant."

"Like what?" He called out in frustration.

Toolas' exasperated chuckle echoed as she walked out of the room. "Use your imagination!" She suggested, closing her office door behind her.

Krac stood still wondering what in the hell that was supposed to mean. Use his imagination? He did not have an imagination. He thought logically. He mapped out the best possible solution to a situation and conducted a very decisive attack. Skeeter was the one with the imagination. She saw life in color while he saw it in black and white. She was twinkling lights and pink freighters. He was... shadows.

"I do not have an imagination," he whispered, holding Skeeter securely in his arms.

Skeeter shook her head and sniffed. "Everyone has an imagination," she whispered as she laid her cheek against his broad chest, feeling safe and warm. "You just haven't discovered yours yet."

"Are your eyes still leaking?" He asked gruffly.

She bit her lip and shook her head. "No," she choked out, pressing her wet face into the opening of his shirt.

Krac released a heavy sigh. "We need to leave. There is much to be done. We have a long trip ahead of us," he murmured, ignoring her lie.

"Where are we going?" She sniffed.

"We are going to Sallas," he replied.

Skeeter frowned and stiffened before pulling back to stare up at him. "Why? I don't have any orders for there. The cargo I have is for Newport. Besides, daddy is on Sallas," she said nervously.

"I know," he said, bending and picking her up in his arms. "That is why we are going there."

"But," she whispered. "I don't want to go to Sallas."

"Why?" Krac asked, striding out of the medical unit. They would take his starship back to the freighter. He could dock it in the lower bay for the journey to Sallas. "It is the most logical place to take you. You will be safe there."

Skeeter ignored the last part. It was not her safety she was worried about, it was his. "Daddy will see you," she said, biting her lip. "He'll know that I… that we… that I…"

Krac paused to look down into her worried eyes. He breathed a sigh of relief that while her eyes were still red and puffy, they no longer leaked. Toolas had been right about giving Skeeter something else to think about.

"Yes," he said with a satisfied nod.

"Yes? Yes? Do you have any idea of what my father will do if he knows that I… that we… He's going to kill you," she replied with a deep sigh and her eyes filled with tears again.

Krac frowned in frustration. He would NOT let her leak again. He stepped into the lift when it opened and turned. The moment the doors closed, he pressed his hand to the control panel and halted it.

"No, he will not kill me," he murmured, setting her down so he could cup her face with his hands. "I will tell him you belong to me now. He will accept it."

Skeeter's mouth dropped open as she stared up at him. Krac noted that at least it cleared her eyes again. He would just have to keep her occupied. That seemed to fix the problem of her tears.

"You're going to tell him I belong to you? Just like that. And you think he'll just accept it. Just like that," she said.

"Yes," he replied confidently.

"Just like that," she repeated.

"Yes, just like that," he replied with a frown at the sound of doubt in her voice.

Skeeter slowly shook her head back and forth. "He's going to kill you," she replied heavily. "Dead. Completely. Totally. Without mercy, dead."

Krac lifted her chin, forcing her to look into his determined eyes. "No, he will accept it," he whispered huskily before he pressed his lips to hers.

Skeeter melted the moment their lips touched. Her hands moved up to his broad shoulders before curling around his neck. She sighed as he parted his lips for her. Warmth filled her as he opened for her. Her hands tightened in his hair when she felt the hardness pressed against her stomach, making her gasp as he pushed her back against the wall of the lift. His lips began moving along her jaw with a desperate urgency that left a burning path that left her hungry.

"Every time I get near you I begin to ache," he muttered as ran his lips back along her jaw to the corner of her mouth. "Feel me! I can shut my body down with a single command, except when I am near you. When you touched me with your lips the other day…." He closed his eyes and released a low hissing breath as he pressed his hips more firmly against her. "I have never experienced anything like that before. No female has ever touched me like that before."

Skeeter tilted her head to the side as his lips slid back down in a fiery path that had her wriggling as the heat exploded between her legs. It took a moment for his words to sink in. She closed her eyes when he opened his mouth and latched onto her throat in a hot wet kiss that pulled a long, low moan from her.

"Oh Krac," she whispered as her fingers frantically pulled at him as she lifted her leg to wind around his. "You make me ache too."

Krac pulled back far enough to look down at her with eyes blazing with desire. He reached down and wrapped his hand around the thigh of the leg pulling him forward. He lifted her slightly so he could press into her more firmly. He groaned as his cock fitted tightly against her. A shudder wracked his body as an almost primitive need flared to life inside him. He slid both of his hands under her ass, forcing her to lift her legs until they were wound around his waist.

"This feels right," he muttered. "I don't understand, but this feels right."

Skeeter's head dropped forward as he rocked against her. Her breathing turned to pants. She couldn't believe this would be her second time with him and she was about to climax in her pants again.

"I need more," Krac growled in frustration as he pushed into her. "Make the ache go away. Like you did before."

"Ah, Krac," an amused male voice interrupted over the comlink in the lift. "I hate to tell you this, but we need the lift. Can you finish this later?"

Skeeter gasped and turned bright red. "They can hear us?"

"Just the last part," the voice chuckled.

Krac closed his eyes and gritted his teeth before opening them again in frustration. "Cooraan, you are a dead man the next time I see you."

Cooraan's laughter echoed in the small compartment. "Just be thankful I was the one that was informed of the malfunction to the lift and not the regular maintenance crew. You might have had more of an audience."

Skeeter tilted her head and frowned. "Do I know you? Your voice sounds awfully familiar."

Cooraan's choked cough covered his muttered curse. "I've reactivated the lift. Safe travels to Sallas."

Krac's eyes flashed at the reminder of the private dance that Skeeter had given the Zion warrior. He released a frustrated sigh and leaned his forehead against Skeeter's when the lift began moving again. He still ached.

"I swear I know him from somewhere," Skeeter murmured in confusion.

"You will forget about him," Krac said, slowly releasing her legs and stepping back. "I want you to tell me how to stop this constant ache. I have never had it before I met you. It is beginning to drive me insane."

Skeeter's mouth dropped open for the second time in astonishment as Krac stepped out of the lift onto the departure bay. Her eyes shimmered in wonder as he pulled her along beside him. She shook her head in disbelief before a mischievous smile lit up her face.

Chapter 22

Skeeter settled back in the co-pilot's seat of Krac's starship. It was much fancier than the freighter's bridge. There were so many lights and panels and screens that it made her head hurt to think about trying to figure out what they all did much less how to fly the damn thing. She knew she should be impressed and ask questions about it, but all she could think about was his softly growled demand in the lift.

She twirled a strand of her thick red hair around her finger and bit her lip. She listened as he received clearance from the *Conqueror* to depart. She glanced out the front viewport as the starship rose before shooting forward out of the side of the Zion Warship.

Darkness surrounded them as they left the brightly lit interior of the warship. The starship tilted slightly as it turned toward the *Lulu Belle*. Skeeter sat forward and stared at her freighter as it came into sight.

She looked at it with a critical eye. It was hard to tell that it was pink in space. It was funny how it ended up that way. It had been a dull dark gray before the explosion that took out almost seven meters of the upper cargo bay on the port side.

"I can't believe I landed that by myself," she murmured.

"I can't either," Krac responded darkly. "If your father had not killed your co-pilot, I would have."

Skeeter shook her head and sighed. "Druss wasn't a very nice man. I caught him stealing from some of the merchants and he... he almost killed a man on one of our stops. He was mean when he was drunk, which was most of the time."

"Why did you keep him on?" He asked with a frown.

She shrugged. "I was going to replace him when we got back to Sallas. He had smuggled illegal cargo aboard that I didn't know about until I found it when I went to scan the inventory for our arrival. He threatened to kill me if I said anything. I guess he planned on moving the canisters, but got drunk halfway through. One broke loose. When it hit the side, the *Lulu Belle* shook like crazy. I issued a mayday and requested emergency planet side assistance as I was losing pressure from the structural damage and had lost my starboard stabilizers. It was too dangerous to try to dock with the Space station as I didn't have enough control."

"Froget said Druss took your escape pod," Krac said before silently wishing he had kept his statement to himself when he saw the flash of pain and sadness reappear in Skeeter's eyes.

Skeeter gave him a sad smile. "Yes. I guess he figured if he escaped and I crashed the *Lulu Belle* there would be no evidence of what happened and no one to point their finger at him. He would take care of both problems at once."

"But you didn't crash," Krac said with a nod.

"No, I didn't crash. I don't know how I made it down in one piece. I think it was the simulator daddy made me do over and over. I liked it. It was like a game. Daddy was on the other end, talking to me the whole time. I focused on what he was saying. He promised to always keep me safe and he has," she replied softly, looking at the *Lulu Belle* with a smile as they got closer.

"Why pink?" Krac asked suddenly, staring at the freighter with a look of horrid fascination.

Skeeter's delighted laughter echoed as she gazed ahead. "There was a mix up with the maintenance crew that was doing the repairs. One brother wanted it painted white. The other wanted it red. They found out they didn't have enough of either to paint the entire thing so they had the bright idea to mix the paint together. Of course, daddy was horrified, but I loved it. There was just enough red paint left over for me to paint the Phoenix on the side as a symbol for surviving my first almost crash."

"He should have killed the brothers as well," Krac reflected before tilting his head to the side. "Maybe not, it does look like you."

"Mm, why do you say that?" She asked, looking at him in surprise.

"It is colorful, like you. The bird on the side is vivid and strong, like you. It is... different, like you," he finished in a husky voice. "I am aching again."

"I know how to take the ache away," Skeeter whispered.

Krac's eyes flashed to hers. The warmth in them sent a shiver through him. The look in her eyes was the same as what he saw in Gracie's when she looked at Kordon. It was a look that he never thought to see from a female, at least not when they looked at him.

His throat tightened as he turned back to open the lower cargo bay doors on the *Lulu Belle*. He entered the opening smoothly and landed. His hands skimmed over the controls, shutting everything down and securing it before he turned in his seat in determination.

"Show me," he demanded in a husky voice. "Show me how you can take the ache away."

"Here?" Skeeter asked, looking at the cramped space before shaking her head. "What I'm planning is going to take a lot more space and you in the horizontal position."

"Horizontal position," he repeated with a frown. "You took the ache away in the vertical position before."

Skeeter's eyes danced with delight. "Krac, can I ask you something personal?"

"Will answering you get you to take the ache away faster?" He asked in frustration as his eyes kept straying to her lips and images of them wrapped around him.

"Oh, definitely," she replied with a shy smile.

"Then yes," he grunted out as she bit her lip again, pulling a low moan from him. "But hurry. I do not like this ache. It is getting worse."

"Have you ever made love to a woman before?" She blurted out, unable to think of a better way to ask him.

"You mean have sex with one?" He asked, cautiously.

Skeeter gave a nervous chuckle. "Sex, made love, got down and dirty, you know," she muttered, blushing.

Krac stiffened before he remembered his promise. "No. My… past," he broke off and looked away. "There was only one time that I had the opportunity to experience sex with a female. My body did not react to her. She was very unpleasant."

* * *

Skeeter rose out of her seat so she could cup his strong face between her hands. It broke her heart to see the flash of doubt in his eyes before he turned away from her. She gently traced his face as he turned back to look at her.

She didn't say anything at first. He was the most unique, most incredible male she had ever met besides Bulldog. Her fingers gently skimmed his brow before tracing over his high cheekbones and down to his jaw.

"I'm glad," she whispered, sliding her hands down so she could entwine her fingers with his. "Do you have a sleeping compartment on-board?"

"Yes, but…." He stood up as she pulled on him. "I like your sleeping quarters better. It is more pleasing."

"Then, my quarters it is. Can you set the auto-pilot?" She asked, pulling him toward the exit.

"I already did," he replied sheepishly. "As soon as we boarded the starship I connected with the *Lulu Belle*. I told you I ache."

She giggled as he stepped down and reached up for her. Instead of setting her down on her feet, he cradled her in his arms as he turned to stride down the corridor toward her room.

She sighed as she snuggled closer. Her mind refused to focus on anything but how she was going to drive him crazy with pleasure. One idea after another swept through her mind. Each one making her hotter than the one before.

"I want to undress you," she murmured, twirling her fingers in the hair along the back of his neck. "Yes, first I'm going to undress you. Slowly. I think I'll kiss every part of you as I do. Mmm, you taste so good. I can't wait to see if the rest of you tastes just as good as your cock. Then, I'm going to explore every inch of you."

"Son-of-a-bitch," Krac cursed hoarsely as he turned the corner. "You are going to kill me if you keep talking like that."

"Just wait until I get my hands on you," she whispered, pressing a hot kiss to his neck. "And my mouth. Definitely my mouth."

* * *

Krac's brain was close to short-circuiting. The images her words were creating, especially after having experienced some of what she was talking about, had his body pulsing with expectation. He swept through the door of her cabin and froze as the unfamiliar feelings of indecision and being unsure of what he should do next hit him. His eyes moved to the bed as he tried to decide what to do next.

He wished now that he had paid more attention to what the guards at the lab had said when they joked around with each other. He knew what sex was by definition. As it had never really applied to him except for that one time in the lab, he had assumed it was a defect in his creation. What he was feeling now made him realize that he was in no way defective. At least, if the hardness of his cock was any indication.

"I... I don't...," he started to say, a confused and uncertain frown making his cheeks turn darker as he gazed down at her.

"It's okay," she whispered, cupping his face with her right hand and stroking his cheek with her thumb. "We'll take it slow. Just let yourself feel."

He slowly lowered her to her feet until she was standing in front of him. He looked down at her with uncertainty. He knew what he wanted to do. Some instinct inside him wanted to rip her clothes off and bury himself deep inside her. He just didn't know if that was his human instinct or his Alluthan. The last thing he wanted to do was scare or hurt her.

He clenched his hands at his side to keep from reaching for her. Sweat beaded on his brow and he wondered vaguely if there might be a problem with the environmental system. His whole body felt hot and his clothes actually felt like they were irritating his skin.

He hissed when he felt the front of his shirt slowly part and Skeeter's hot, moist lips pressing against his chest. He held himself stiff, afraid that if he touched her, she would stop. His throat worked up and down as her lips moved further down as she released more of the buttons on his shirt.

"Skeeter, I am not sure this is... perhaps we should..." his voice faded to a low moan as she slid his shirt off his shoulders. "That feels incredible."

"How about this?" She asked as she teased his left nipple with her tongue. "Or this?" She pulled the clasp holding the front of his pants loose and slid her hands down and around him so she could cup his ass.

"Yes!" His loud moan filled her room. "Skeeter, I want to touch you."

"Then do it," she replied huskily, looking up at his taut face. "Touch me, Krac. Touch me any way you want."

"I want to rip your clothes off of you," he admitted, his cheeks turning dark again. "I am afraid of scaring you."

Skeeter's eyes lit up and a mischievous smile curled her lips as she pulled back just far enough for him to have room to touch her. If he thought wanting to rip her clothes off her would scare her, she wondered what he would think if she told him she wanted to tie him up and have her wicked way with him. She had a feeling that her idea of going slow was about to be blasted into hyperspace.

"I've always wanted a guy who could rip my clothes off me," she said, tilting her head to the side. "I think that would be incredibly sexy."

Her eyes widened in surprise as the sound of cloth tearing echoed in the room before she even finished her sentence. Her lips formed an 'O' as her lacy bra followed her shirt. She moaned loudly when his calloused hands cupped her heavy breasts and lifted them.

"Oh my God, you learn fast," she panted as his lips captured her right nipple and he sucked deeply on it. "Oh baby, yessss!"

"I like this," he growled as he released her nipple and moved to the other.

"You aren't the only one," Skeeter moaned as her eyes closed as he kneaded her breasts as he sucked on her nipple. His thumb and forefinger rolled her other one between them. "I refuse to come in my pants again. Naked, you – me now!"

Krac pulled back with a hot glare before he gripped her around the waist and tossed her onto her bed. He pushed his pants down, kicking off his boots and pulled them off. His eyes never left Skeeter, who was watching him with her own hot look.

He stepped closer to the bed and bent to grip the top of her pants. It was a good thing she was wearing a pair from medical. The waist was elastic and he gripped it and her panties at the same time. Her slippered shoes came off with her pants.

"You are so beautiful," he bit out in a hoarse voice.

"You aren't so bad yourself," she replied, licking her lips as she watched his long, thick and very, very hard cock jerk up and down. "Not bad at all."

"I want to taste you," he said, staring down at the rich dark red curls that covered her mound.

Skeeter relaxed back with a happy sigh. She had died and gone to heaven. She had been sneaking romance stories and vidcoms for years with Tila's help. She had always dreamed of finding a male who would talk dirty and want to make love the way the heroes and heroines did in the stories.

"Go for it. I'm all yours," she whispered.

"Of course you are. I will never let you go. That is why your father will accept it when I tell him," Krac replied arrogantly.

She released an exasperated sigh and shook her head. "Word of advice," she chuckled, looking him in the eye. "Don't mention my dad when we are making love. That is the surest way to kill the mood."

His eyes widened before he nodded his head. "I do not want that. I want this," he said, kneeling next to the bed so he could touch her soft curls.

"Oh baby yes," she sighed as his fingers ran through the soft thatch. Her hips tilted upward when he tugged on it and she lifted her left leg to wrap it around his shoulder. "I'm on fire for you."

Krac's eyes jerked up to her face at her softly whispered words. The sweet sound was like a calming balm for his soul. Her face was flushed and her hands were over her head, causing the rounded mounds of her breasts to lift. Her nipples stood rosy and taut from his lips.

He looked back down and ran his fingers through her thick curls again. Each time he did, she would moan and her hips would move. Heated fascination held him mesmerized as his fingers ran down along the slick folds hiding her womanhood. His eyes flashed up to her face when she moaned louder and tilted her hips more, as if seeking his touch.

He focused back on his exploration. He wanted to know everything about her. He wanted to learn how to make her moan and to bring her the same pleasure that she brought to him. He ran his fingers over the small nub before he pushed deeply inside her silky channel. He flushed with heated pleasure at her loud cry.

"You are so soft and smooth," he whispered as her hips rocked back and forth.

"Please," she panted, clutching at the top of her bed. "Like that."

Krac leaned forward as her leg tightened around his shoulder. He parted her slick lips and pressed his mouth against the swollen nub. The moment he did, sweet ambrosia flooded him. Molten lava poured through his system as his senses reacted to her desire. He ran his tongue over the nub enjoying how it swelled for him. Skeeter's loud cries and heavy panting told him that she was enjoying what he was doing.

He stroked her, pushing his long fingers deep into her while he continued teasing her. Her body reacted by sending more of her sweet juice over his lips and tongue. His body grew impossibly harder, but some instinct told him it was important to bring her to pleasure first. He dipped his tongue into her before roughly stroking over her nub again. He was rewarded when her body froze and she exploded, sending a wave of sweet moisture around his fingers and lips.

"Oh God! Oh God! Oh God!" She chanted over and over as she wrapped her legs around him and held him pressed tightly against her for several long seconds before she reluctantly released him. "That was... incredible," she choked out, opening her eyes to look at him in stunned disbelief.

"More," he grunted, rising up. "I hurt."

* * *

Skeeter's arms wrapped around him as he crawled up her body to seal his lips to hers. The taste of herself on his lips sent a wave of possessiveness through her that she didn't know she was capable of feeling. This huge, awesome male was hers, all hers.

She lifted her legs and wrapped them around his waist. The move pressed his hard cock against her slick core. She moaned as his hips flexed instinctively. The movement pushed the bulbous head of his cock inside her pulling another moan as his cock slid along her sensitive vaginal channel. The feel of his cock stretching her, filling her, sent a wave of intense pleasure through her.

Her arms tightened around him when his large frame shuddered and stiffened. She reluctantly allowed him to pull back, breaking their heated kiss. A knowing smile curved her lips at the heated look of surprise on his face before a more determined expression transformed it as he pushed a little deeper.

"Oh yes. That's it," she whispered, scraping her fingernails along his scalp and rocking her hips so that he moved deeper into her. "You feel soooo good."

"Skeeter," he panted, pushing deeper before pulling back so he could do it again. "I… this is… I feel like I'm going to explode."

"I can't wait until you do," she whispered, tightening her legs around his waist and rocking. "Go faster. Wait until you do that. Faster and deeper."

His face was taut with emotion as he did as she said. His arms strained as he held himself off of her for fear of crushing her. He stared down into her face as he moved his hips. His lips parted when he pulled back and drove as far as he could into her.

"Ohhh!" He moaned as she wrapped tightly around his throbbing length. "I… have… to…. I have… to… deeper… faster."

"Yes to both," she moaned.

Krac lowered himself so he could wrap his arms around her soft curves. His broad hands spread across her back, pulling her against his chest as he buried his face in her neck. He shivered as her hands curved around him, holding him to her as he moved.

He pulled in gasping breaths as he drove into her. His eyes closed as he felt a strange tingling begin. He swore his balls were about to explode they were so tight. The feel of her fisting his shaft, stroking it, sent wave after wave of intense pleasure through him.

He felt her short nails clawing at his back as he moved faster. Her loud cry echoed through the room as her body locked around him. The intensity of her pulsing around his cock lifted him to a new level of pleasure/pain that shattered the taut string holding him back. His body erupted into her with a force that had him arching upward, straining.

"Yessss," he groaned out, pulsing into her as he ground his hips against hers. "Oh yes."

* * *

Skeeter looked up at his tense features. His eyes were closed, his lips slightly parted as he drew in rasping breaths. His brow was drawn as the power of what just happened still held him in its grasp. The muscles in his neck stood out and he shuddered as another wave struck him as he came down from his climax. It was the most beautiful sight she had ever seen.

Running her hands up his forearms, she waited until his head fell forward and he opened his eyes to stare down at her in stunned silence. She smiled tenderly up at the wild look of passion that still ensnared him. She gently stroked his arms and shoulders before touching his cheek with the tips of her fingers.

"I love you, Krac," she murmured softly. "You make me feel safe, happy and whole."

Krac's eyes darkened at her words. "You are mine, Lulu Belle. No one, no one will take you from me."

Her eyes glittered as he used her real name for the first time. She gently pulled him down to her so she could seal her lips over his. A soft moan escaped when she felt him move inside her.

It would appear he is a very, very fast learner, she thought happily as he started to move again.

Chapter 23

Skeeter had been nervous about returning to the *Lulu Belle* but Krac made sure she was kept too busy over the next several days to let the memories of what happened overwhelm her. When they weren't making love, he was asking her a million and one questions about her life. Where she had grown up, what she liked to do and why was the freighter filled with so many strange objects. She had happily answered his questions, but it troubled her that every time she asked some of the same questions about him, he would change the subject or distract her.

During that time, he also showed her the updated equipment that had been installed by the engineering crew aboard the *Conqueror*. She listened as he gave her a detailed tour of the new security and defense systems that was installed. She smiled and nodded, but most of what he was saying went over her head.

"Why would I need those?" Skeeter asked, pointing to the laser defense grid showing on the console in front of her. "I didn't even know that the *Lulu Belle* had laser cannons."

"I can't believe your dad let you out into space without a working defense system," Krac muttered darkly. "Didn't you do a maintenance check on them?"

"Oh, well, they probably did work when I got the *Lulu Belle*," she began, biting at her lower lip. "Terry told me not to worry about it. He said he would take care of it."

"This is the male that you belonged to," Krac growled.

Skeeter scowled at him. "I didn't 'belong' to him."

"He became your lover," he countered in a low voice.

"More out of curiosity and boredom," she retorted. "It was a mistake. Everyone is entitled to at least one. Count him as mine."

"What about the dance you gave to Cooraan, Bran and Rorrak? Was that a mistake as well?" He snapped out, glaring at her.

Skeeter's eyes opened wide as everything clicked. "That's where I knew him from! I knew it. I did recognize his voice," she muttered in disbelief before her eyes widened even further at Krac's dark expression. She burst out laughing. "You're jealous," she breathed.

"I am not jealous," he muttered, looking down at the controls. "You danced for them."

"I didn't know that it was 'that' kind of place. Druss just told me that some guys were interested in the dance I had learned. I thought they wanted to know how to do it," she muttered. "I ended up knocking two of them out by mistake. I didn't know the stick I had was that long or that they were sitting so close. I was really into the dance. It is very empowering," she mumbled.

Krac's lips twitched before a low laugh escaped him. "Bran said you almost emasculated Roarrk."

Skeeter's soft laugh combined with his. "You should have seen their eyes when I started the dance," she giggled. "I don't think they were quite expecting me to start shouting, or beating my chest before I grabbed the stick. Before I knew it this one guy jumps up at the same time as I swung around. His eyes were bugging out further than mine when I caught him in his you-know-what!"

The picture Skeeter was painting in his mind drew more laughter out of Krac. Before he knew what was happening, he found Skeeter's warm, curvy body sitting on his lap with her arms wrapped tightly around his neck. The laughter died on his lips as she gently skimmed his face with the tips of her fingers.

"You have the most beautiful laugh," she whispered, leaning forward to press her lips against his. "I ache."

His eyes warmed as she pulled back. "I know how to take the ache away," he murmured, his eyes alight with desire.

"Show me," she breathed out, winding her arms around his neck and pressing her lips against his again with a desperate hunger.

His arms tightened around her. He blindly felt for the console and connected with it briefly. He sent a brief command before he disconnected so he could rise out of the chair with her in his arms. His eyes flickered up long enough to guide them down the corridor to her cabin.

He broke the kiss as he laid her down on the bed. His hands worked frantically at her shirt. He growled in frustration before just tearing it open. His lips caressed the swell of her bare breast as he bent over her. He had insisted when they dressed earlier that she didn't need to wear the torture device that bound her. He liked the way her nipples stood out against the fabric without it.

"I swear I can't get enough of you," she cried out as he moved down her body.

"Spread your legs," he demanded, ripping the sides of her boxers.

"I'm not going to have any clothes left if you keep tearing them up," she informed him as she lifted her ass up far enough for him to toss the tattered remains to the floor.

"Good," he muttered, causing his heated breath to caress the soft curls between her legs. "I like you without clothes on."

"I like me without clothes on too," she moaned as her legs fell apart. "Especially when you are doing this to me."

"Good," he repeated as he pulled her toward the edge of the bed.

"Oh so good," she breathed out as the world began to shatter around her.

* * *

Pleasure exploded through Krac as he pressed his lips against the small nub he discovered made her say and do wild things. He ran his tongue over it, moaning as sweet ambrosia touched his lips. He slid his hands up under her thighs and lifted her legs up over his shoulders wanting more.

"Wait!" She panted, staring up blindly at the ceiling.

"No," he grunted, wrapping his hands around her thighs to hold her still while he continued to tease her.

"I... oh god, I... wanted... to... show you... something new," she moaned out. "It will be so good. I promise."

Krac reluctantly pulled back just far enough that she could feel his heated breath against her throbbing core. She could tell he was thinking. She wanted to show him that there were many ways they could make love.

"Just as good?" He demanded, suspicious.

"Better," she promised, tilting her head up so she could see him. "Much, much better."

"I don't think that is possible," he confessed. "What you do to me... it is... incredible."

Her face softened at the look of vulnerability that chased across his face for just a moment as he admitted his feelings. Her heart melted when she thought of how different his life must have been compared to the other men she had known. He was just... adorable to her.

"There are so many ways we can pleasure each other. I want to try them all with you," she said.

"Many? How many?" He asked, suddenly looking anything but vulnerable. He looked more like a predator seeing his prey being offered on a platter.

"I don't know," she laughed softly. "I guess we'll just have to count them as we discover them."

"Show me another way," he demanded, pulling back.

Skeeter gazed up at him as he stood next to the bed. Her eyes ran hungrily down his tall form, freezing on his long shaft that pulsed up and down. The tip of his cock was darker with his desire and a light touch of pre-cum glistened from it. She held her hand out to him.

"Come here," she whispered.

The moment he placed his hand in hers, she jerked on it, pulling him off balance. She rolled to the side as he twisted, landing on his back on the bed. His eyes were wide with surprise before they darkened to almost black as she rose up over him and straddled his face while running her full breasts along his chest.

She looked down between them and smiled as she widened her legs just a touch more before lowering herself over his lips. She moaned as she felt his head rise up to meet her. Her own hands moved down to wrap around his cock. She held it steady as she wiped her tongue over the end.

"Fuck!"

Skeeter smiled at his hoarse exclamation. She slowly began rocking back and forth as she pulled him into her mouth while she rode him. The deep groan and the swelling of his cock in her hands told her that he was definitely enjoying this.

She was too. The combination of having him pleasure her while she sucked deeply on him was too much for her already primed body. The wave of her climax caught her off guard and she splintered into a million pieces of delicious, molten pleasure.

She pulled back with a loud cry when he continued to grip her thighs, holding her while he stroked her clit over and over, drawing out her orgasm. Unable to fight against the explosive pleasure still wracking her body, she fell forward, sinking her teeth into his thigh as she came again hard. It took several long seconds before she realized what she had done. She pressed a heated kiss to the imprint she had left as her body continued to shake from the aftermath of her orgasms

"More," he growled.

"Yes, more," she whispered hoarsely, trying to push herself up. She ran her tongue around the throbbing head of his cock before she forced her leg over his head. "Much more."

"Where are you going?" He demanded as she turned back around until she was facing him. "I liked that view."

Skeeter slid her leg over his waist. "I did too but I like watching your face when you come. It is incredibly sexy."

"I... yes, this is good too," he hissed as she slowly impaled herself on him. "Very good."

"Touch me," she moaned as she rose up and sank back down. "God, you are so thick and long."

Krac's hands rose up to cup her full breasts. He liked how her nipples hardened as he ran his thumb over them. The shudder of her body and the way she tightened around his cock spurred him to draw one of them down to his lips.

"Oh yes, baby. Like that, just like that," she whispered, moving her hips in a slight circle as she moved up and down. "Together, push them together and suck on them."

Krac watched as her face flushed again and her eyes closed as he pushed her breasts together and drew both of her nipples into his mouth. He sucked deeply on them before rolling his tongue around the hard tips.

Pleasure poured through him when he felt her hands tighten on his shoulders as she leaned forward. This position allowed him to go deeper into her. He drove upwards as she was coming down on him. Her dark blue eyes opened and she stared down at him with in surprise.

"Again," she demanded in a breathless voice that pulled his balls up even harder than they had been. "Do that again."

He sucked hard on her while pulling slowly back out before driving into her again. This time the moan came from him as she clenched her vaginal channel tightly around his cock. He could feel every inch of her slick walls. She tightened around him when he tried to pull back.

He released her breasts, moving his hands down so he could grip her hips instead. His head fell back against the pillows as he stared up into her eyes as he drove into her again. This time he was controlling the rhythm.

"I like this way," he grunted as he picked up the speed. "You are beautiful when you come."

"Krac, I… oh… oh… oh…," she moaned as her body splintered again around his. "It's too much."

"Never," he growled. "It will never be too much."

His eyes remained glued to her flushed face as his hands tightened their grip. His hips moved in a primitive rhythm driven by his desire and need to claim her as his. He gritted his teeth as the tingling started to move through his body. He knew now what was about to happen. The pleasure and release were fast becoming an addiction to him.

He pulled almost all the way out of her, the tip of his cock catching at her slick entrance. He knew this was it. The slight control that he had snapped as he drove into her one last time. Every inch of his cock could feel her hot, wet softness surrounding it, pulsing with her own release. The tip touched her womb and hot semen shot from him, pouring into her as he burst apart in a world of color. A world only she could give him.

His hands shook as he drew her down to lay in drowsy silence on top of him, still connected as one. He held her close to his hammering heart and breathed in the essence of their combined passions. He continued to tenderly stroke her back long after her breathing had calmed and he knew she had fallen into a deep, exhausted sleep.

"No," he murmured, looking up at the twinkling lights of her room and realizing that she had made the ceiling look like the heavens on a clear night. "No, it will never be too much."

* * *

Three days later, things were not so good. Skeeter sighed nervously and pushed impatiently at her hair that kept falling out of the lopsided ponytail that she had hurriedly put it in. She stared down at the dark green and blue planet below with tribulation.

No matter how much she tried to talk him out of it. Krac insisted that they needed to go to Sallas. He also insisted that he needed to speak with her father.

"Your lip is going to be raw if you do not stop biting it," he observed as he made the final arrangements for their arrival.

"I should have told daddy about you," she groaned, shaking her head and biting her lip again. "I should have eased him into the idea. Let him know. Something."

"I told you that. You refused to let me talk to him," he pointed out. "I did not like it when your eyes leaked again. That is the only reason I gave in."

"Maybe you should stay on board the *Lulu Belle* until after I talk to him. You'll be closer to your starship. It is faster if he….," her voice faded at his dark, determined look. "I don't want him to kill you!"

Krac's eyes softened when he saw the shimmer of tears in her eyes and the tremble to her bottom lip as she stared at him in genuine worry and fear. He reached his hand out to her, gently squeezing her fingers in comfort. While he had no desire to fight a full grown, enraged Triterian male, he not only would but he could and win. The biggest problem was he didn't think Skeeter would be happy with him if he killed her beloved father.

"He will accept that you now belong to me," he said instead before letting go of her fingers to finish the landing procedure.

"I hope so," she whispered as they broke through the atmosphere and began the final approach to her father's stronghold. "I really, really hope so."

Chapter 24

"Skeeter, my little shining sun," Bulldog's deep voice echoed from the arrival hanger at the Sallas Space docks. "You are just as beautiful as ever. You are happy, yes? The *Lulu Belle* is…. in one piece!" He said in surprise, looking over the pink hull with distaste. "It still needs new paint."

"Daddy!"

Skeeter couldn't help the huge smile that lit up her face whenever she saw her 'dad'. She ran down the loading platform of the *Lulu Belle* and jumped into his outstretched arms. She loved it when he wrapped his six arms around her and held her up off the ground. It felt as if she was flying.

Even as nervous and frightened as she was about how he was going to react to Krac, old habits die hard. A deep sigh escaped her as he lifted her up in his arms. The soft, red scales covering his body felt warm and smooth as she buried her face into his neck.

"I missed you," she whispered as she closed her eyes and drew in his warm, comforting scent.

"Froget has been a good co-pilot for you? He has done well in keeping you safe?" Bulldog asked with a low rumble of satisfaction.

Emotions overwhelmed her at the sound of Frog's name. Being back home in her dad's safe embrace opened the floodgates as she remembered everything that had happened. Finding Violet, meeting Krac, Frog's death and her almost dying were just a part of it. It was her fear of what he might do to Krac that finally triggered the huge avalanche of feelings she had been barely hanging on to. She fought against the sob that built, but it was too much. Her body shook as she wrapped her arms tightly around Bulldog's neck and clung to him like she did when she was the scared little girl whose parents had been murdered.

"Oh, my Lulu Belle," Bulldog said tenderly, rubbing her back with two of his hands. "My poor, poor sweet girl."

"He… he… killed him," she sobbed. "I tried to… to… stop him, but I had to hide Violet first. I was too… late. Frog… Frog died to save me and Violet. Oh daddy, why? He was so brave and that horrible man kill… killed him."

"Oh, my sunshine," Bulldog murmured, his eyes flashing to the back of the *Lulu Belle* where a huge male stood staring at him with cold, deadly eyes. "I will take care of this."

Skeeter sniffed and clung even tighter to him when she felt his hands begin to move. She pulled back and wiped at her damp cheeks before glancing over her shoulder at where Krac stood on the lowered platform. A shaky apologetic smile curved her lips as she remembered how much he hated it when she 'leaked'.

"Daddy, this is…" She started to say when Bulldog set her gently, but firmly, behind him.

"You dare cause my daughter to cry? You dare cause her to be sad?" Bulldog's deep voice bellowed out in rage. "You dare go near the daughter of Bulldog Ti'Death?"

"Daddy, no! He saved my life! Please, he is... very special to me," Skeeter cried out, holding on to one of her father's hands.

Bulldog's hand tightened on hers, but he didn't turn away from the huge male who stood frozen at the end of the platform. The challenge in the male's eyes was enough to make him want to kill him. But more important, it was the possessive way the male's gaze swept over Lulu Belle that caused him the most concern. This was not a gentle male. This was a cold-blooded killer. And, from the way his eyes focused on Lulu Belle, he had claimed her as his.

"Lulu Belle, go to my transport," Bulldog growled in a low voice.

"I love him, daddy," Skeeter whispered. "He makes me happy. He makes me feel safe. Please don't hurt him."

Bulldog froze at her soft words. He heard the change in her voice when she talked about the male. He glanced down at her. Her eyes were not on him, but on the huge male. He could see the warmth and love in them. He also saw the possessive look when she gazed at him. Bulldog released a deep sigh before turning to pierce the male with a heated look.

"Who are you?" Bulldog asked bluntly. "And how did you meet my daughter?"

* * *

Krac stood on the balcony looking out over the courtyard of the huge villa that Ti'Death had built into the cliffs overlooking the dark green ocean from below. Skeeter told him that Bulldog had the villa built shortly after he brought her back to Sallas. Her father wanted her to have a place where she could grow up safe from many of his business dealings.

"You have the power to break her spirit if you are not careful," Bulldog's deep voice said quietly behind him. "She cares for you. When she loves, she loves deeply."

Krac glanced over his shoulder as the Triterian male warily approached him. They had called a silent truce back at the arrival platform. He knew it wouldn't last. They were both two very dominant males and they both loved the same female; one as a male loves his female, the other as a father loves his daughter.

"She is mine. I will protect and care for her," he replied, turning back to gaze down at the courtyard where Skeeter talked animatedly with several of the house helpers.

Bulldog's deep sigh echoed quietly as he came to stand next to him. Both of them watched as two other males carried a large crate to the center of a flower bed. After several minutes of struggling, the crate was opened to reveal a brilliant sculpture.

Three large circles, with multiple smaller circles within them spun around as the sailing ships in the center of each circle caught the light breeze spinning them. As they spun, the sun caught the colorful glass that was positioned throughout the circles.

"She is very special," Bulldog murmured. "She sees the beauty and good in things that others don't. Everything she touches comes to life. I have done my best to protect her from the darkness that fills the universe."

Krac's hands tightened on the balcony as he heard the caution in Bulldog's voice. His eyes were focused on her beautiful smile as she nodded to one of the women standing near her. His throat tightened when she looked up to where he and Bulldog were standing. Her smile faltered for a moment before it returned, softer and warmer than before.

"She is very special," he agreed quietly.

"Everyone has always feared me," Bulldog stated quietly. "Even members of my own species. The Triterians are known as much for our blood-thirst as we are for our business sense. As one of the most successful members, I have had to do things that are often frowned upon by some planetary councils, including the Confederation."

"You are a lead councillor for your own star system. As such, the council listens to you," Krac responded. "And looks the other way."

Bulldog chuckled and folded his arms across his massive chest. "At times, it was necessary and prudent if they did not want a war on their hands. You have done your homework, Section K."

Krac stiffened at his identification section. "I am not the only one, it would seem," he said in a quiet menacing voice.

"Does my daughter know who you really are?" Bulldog asked point blank.

Krac's knuckles turned white from where he was gripping the stone railing before he forced himself to relax. He breathed deeply to control the unfamiliar rush of panic that threatened to choke him. His eyes moved upward until he was staring sightlessly out over the brilliant green of the ocean.

"No," he replied in a short, quiet tone.

Bulldog studied the unusual male's stiff form. He saw the proud, powerful jaw clench, as if waiting for him to attack. He saw a man of power. A man who lived by a code of honor he alone understood. This was a man whom many considered a monster. It was a title he was familiar with. A slow smile curved his lips as he glanced back down at his beautiful but unusual daughter.

"Tell her," Bulldog suggested. "You will be surprised by her reaction. As I said before, she sees things others do not."

Krac didn't say anything at first. In truth, a part of him was stunned to hear the quiet acceptance in Bulldog's voice. He had expected threats, even a possible attempt to kill him. Not this acceptance.

"I need to ask you a favor," he said gruffly. "I have to leave. There is a… situation that requires my attention. I ask that you protect her until I return."

Bulldog studied the tight expression on Krac's face. "Does this have anything to do with the New Order and their attacks on the Earth's council?" He asked in a voice suddenly cool and reserved.

Krac's eyes narrowed in suspicion. "What do you know of the New Order and their attacks?"

"You are not the only one concerned," Bulldog replied with a sigh. "I know more than you can imagine. All is not what it seems. I have ways of knowing what is going on. It is not only the Earth that is in danger should the council change. I have been observing some suspicious requests for items."

"What type of items?" Krac asked.

"Anything pertaining to the Alluthans. Someone has been searching for anything about them, including debris from their ships, vidcom on them, even bodies."

"The Confederation Council and the Zion military have control over that," Krac stated.

"There is always those who are willing to exchange illegal items if the price is right. The New Order is searching for something. What, I do not know yet. But, they are searching for something," Bulldog said grimly.

Krac's mind raced as he tried to piece together what Bulldog was telling him with the information he already had. Why would the New Order want to know about the Alluthans? Why did they want Gracie Jones-Jefe? Frustration ate at him.

Harden had been working for Tillman's corporation. He had delivered materials, supposedly mining equipment and basic defense weapons, to the mining colonies along the outer rims. Those were the ones the Alluthan's attacked. Yet, there had only been the one Mothership. It had been destroyed and the remaining items collected by the Confederation's top scientists to study. Everything Gracie knew had been recorded. He knew because he had tapped into the

Confederation's computer database and downloaded everything they had discovered.

His eyes flickered to where Skeeter had been. He frowned as his eyes searched for her. He turned when he heard her soft laughter coming from the room behind them.

"I need your promise you will keep her safe until I return," Krac muttered under his breath as Skeeter stepped out onto the balcony.

"I gave her that promise long before I give it to you," Bulldog replied. "I would start on Pryus. The parts store held more than Violet Jefe."

"How do you know that?" Krac asked in surprise.

"Because you are not the only unusual male that was created in the labs. Another of your kind was searching for something there as well according to my sources," Bulldog murmured before he stepped forward with a wide grin and pulled Skeeter into his arms for another hug.

Krac watched as the Triterian asked Skeeter about the new sculpture she had designed. His own heart warmed when her eyes kept searching out him even as his mind ran through the data pouring through it. He nodded and his lips curved up at the corners when her shy smile of relief sent a flush of happiness to her cheeks that he and her father had talked and not tried to kill each other.

Chapter 25

"Why? Why can't I go with you?" Skeeter asked in frustration the next morning as they stood next to his sleek starship that had been readied for departure. "I can help."

"You faint at the sight of blood. If things work out the way I suspect, there will be a lot of it," Krac reminded her.

"But... what if you need help?" She asked worriedly. "What if you get hurt?"

Krac paused at the sound of fear and worry in her voice. It was taking every ounce of his self-control to leave her here. Her safety meant more to him than his own fear of leaving her. She would be safe here with Bulldog. She would be in danger as long as she was with him, especially if what Bulldog told him proved correct.

He had no idea that others of his kind had survived. He had been under the impression that all other models had been destroyed by the scientists at the labs before Anastasia's team could rescue them. His mind swept over his conversation early this morning with Roarrk and Anastasia. Another attempt had been made on her life. She had been wounded but refused to let it stop her.

"They are getting desperate. This attack happened in broad daylight in the center of town," Roarrk growled.

"Anastasia, what do you know about the other Alluthan clones at the facilities you raided? Do you know if any others of my kind were freed?" Krac demanded.

Anastasia bit her lip before staring him in the eye. Her face was bruised and dark circles under her eyes highlighted her exhaustion. It took several moments before she finally answered him.

"Yes," she answered softly. "There are others."

"Why wasn't I told?" He demanded coldly.

"Krac," Roarrk warned.

"No, Roarrk. He deserves to know. I take full responsibility," she replied softly before turning back to Krac. "There were a total of five Allbreeds that we know of that survived. Six, now, if what Bulldog told you is true. You and four others were rescued. At first, we weren't sure if you could link with the others. It was decided it was best to keep you isolated from each other to see. Two of the Allbreed escaped shortly after they were separated. We believe they could link together and communicate with each other. Their escapes were very well coordinated and it is believed they are together."

"And the other two?" He asked stiffly. "What became of them?"

"One was killed when he attacked several of the scientists. The other... the other was moved to an isolated facility where she could live in a safe environment."

"She?!" Krac whispered in disbelief. "A female?"

Anastasia sighed and leaned back against Roarrk as he wrapped his arm around her. "Yes. From the little we could find out, she was considered a surprise to those at the facility. As far as we can tell, there was never any record of the Alluthans having female offspring. The research showed that all attempts to clone a female had failed until Section A was created."

"What about this sixth one?" He demanded. "How was he not discovered?"

"He must have either been taken from the facility before it was destroyed or..." Her voice faded for a moment as her eyes darkened. "Or... there was a cover up by one of my teams."

"Find out which it was. I am headed back to Pryus to see if I can find out what he was looking for," Krac replied.

"Be careful," Anastasia whispered. "I would never hurt you, Krac, not intentionally. I'm sorry I didn't tell you this information before."

Krac could see the sincerity in Anastasia's eyes, but it still burned that she did not trust him, even after he had pledged to protect her and her family. He nodded stiffly before signing off. He had a lot to do before he left. One of which was making sure a certain curvy redhead was kept safe until his return.

He turned when he felt her hand on his arm. A low groan escaped him at the worry in her eyes. He pulled her into his arms and held her close to his heart. His eyes closed as the warmth spread through him. He never expected to find a female to call his own.

He had a better appreciation for Kordon's rage when he kidnapped Gracie. In all honesty, he admired Kordon's restraint in not trying to kill him for putting his mate in such danger. The thought of someone considering Skeeter collateral damage sent piercing waves of pain through him. Bulldog was right. She brought color to his world.

"I will return as soon as I can," he promised in a husky voice. "Stay with your father. I will come for you when my mission is over."

"But... what if you don't come back?" She whispered.

"I will," he vowed, tilting her head so he could brush his lips along hers. "I have something worth coming back for."

Skeeter's lips twitched as she tenderly touched his face. "You'd better or I'll come find you and shoot your ass for making me."

Krac chuckled. "That would be very painful," he teased.

Skeeter's eyes grew serious as she stared up at him. "Just be careful."

"I will. Visit with your father. He missed you as well," Krac said, reluctantly releasing her.

"I'm still in shock you two didn't try to kill each other," she murmured as he bent to pick up a small pack off the ground next to him. "Especially when you told him you were sleeping where I did. I've never seen him turn that dark a red before."

Krac laughed again and shook his head. He had thought for sure that the huge Triterian was about to attack him as well, but instead he just muttered something unintelligible under his breath. He was sure Bulldog had refrained from attacking because of Skeeter. She had been sitting across from her father with a huge, happy grin on her face.

"Are you ready to leave?" Bulldog asked dryly from behind them. "I thought you were in a hurry. I've already approved your clearance to take off."

Skeeter shook her head and sighed in reproach. "Daddy."

Krac nodded to Bulldog when he folded his six arms across his chest and glared at him. From the glaring frown and the impatience in the Triterian's voice, it was obvious he had not been forgiven for sleeping with his daughter. He shrugged his broad shoulders. It may take time but Bulldog was going to have to learn that he was no longer the only male in Skeeter's life.

"Keep her safe," he growled, brushing a hard, possessive kiss across her mouth. "I love you," he whispered as he brushed another kiss near her ear before he turned and walked over to the sleek starship.

Skeeter stood still, her eyes wide as she fought back tears. She wrapped her arms tightly around her waist as she watched the silver ship rise off the ground and turn before it quickly gained altitude and disappeared.

She leaned back against her dad when he protectively wrapped his arms around her. She let her head drop back against his chest and released a sad sigh. Her eyes briefly closed before she opened them with a glitter of determination.

She still had cargo to deliver. If there was one way to cope with fear it was by keeping busy. Tila had taught her that. She would spend a few days with her dad before she finished her original run to Newport.

"So, tell me how Tila is doing," Bulldog said, turning her back toward his private transport. "Is she ready for me to kill Artemis yet so I can bring her back home?"

Skeeter turned and rose up on her toes to kiss him on the cheek. "Not yet," she responded, linking her arm through two of his and squeezing his hand, letting him know she knew he was trying to distract her. "Did you really tear off some of Lucas' fingers?"

"Would I do something like that?" Bulldog asked, trying to look innocent.

He released a contented sigh as Skeeter's infectious laughter rang through the air. *Perhaps I won't have to kill the male after all. She is glowing with happiness,* he thought with satisfaction. *My very, very beautiful little girl has found her mate.*

Chapter 26

Pryus Spaceport: Lower Level

"What have you discovered?" The raspy voice on the other side of the vidcom asked. "Did you find what I sent you for?"

Section L stared back at the cloaked figure with cold, emotionless eyes. "It is not here," he responded.

"It has to be! Search again. Pius said the contact gave it to him," the voice snapped. "I need that item!"

"Pius is dead. The shop was secured, but the item was taken before his death," Section L replied.

Silence met his words before the voice spoke again. "Was it the assassin?"

"No," Section L stated. "I was able to access the lower section security vidcoms. I know who took the item. Do you wish for me to retrieve it?"

"Yes," the raspy voice said. "Terminate whoever took it. Leave no trace."

"Affirmative," Section L replied. "I will contact you when I have the item."

"Don't fail or you will not be the only one terminated," the voice warned before the vidcom went blank.

Section L stared at the dark screen in his hand before carefully sliding it back into his pocket. Only when the device was safely tucked away did he release the control he tried desperately to maintain. It was vital that he retain the unemotional mask, especially when he was reminded of what could happen if he failed, but each threat made it more difficult.

He shook the dust off of his fist as he pulled it from the wall next to him. His eyes swept the cluttered area. He had seen several things in the vidcom that he kept to himself. Soon, he would return with the item and when he did… when he did, he would end the control the Leader had over him once and for all.

Pulling the hood of his cloak over his head, he exited the dark building. He paused briefly to connect with the security vidcom. A satisfied smile curled his lips as he opened his eyes.

The Leader was not the only one with a plan, Section L thought as he disappeared down the dark alley.

* * *

Two weeks later, Krac stood in the same place that he had been when he was searching for Violet. Dust and clutter littered the area worse than it had before. His eyes narrowed on the wall behind the counter.

He gingerly stepped over the items that had been tossed aside, more than likely by the Spaceport authorities during their 'investigation'. He stared at the newly formed hole for several seconds before he turned to see what else had been disturbed. He retrieved the image of the small store from his memory banks and scanned it for additional changes.

His eyes swept over the store carefully. He paused on the area near the wall where a row of shelves were. The imprint of fresh prints in the dust captured his attention. He stepped over to the wall. On the third shelf, the outline of four fingers were clearly visible. There were no fingerprints. Whoever had placed their hand on the shelf had been wearing gloves.

Krac stared at the prints for a moment, trying to see what had held the male's attention. His eyes scanned the shelf when a small object, carefully placed near the wall, caught his attention. He reached into the shadows and wrapped his fingers around the small, black part. He turned it in his hand and frowned. A shiver of unease washed through him as he stared at the navigation module.

A low curse burst from his lips as he saw a touch of yellow paint on one side. A vision of the *Lulu Belle's* console, creatively color coded, flooded his mind, even as Froget's words echoed with it.

"I don't know why she wants to be a freighter captain. She can't pilot one worth a damn. That's why she's got all the buttons color coded, it's to help remind her what they are supposed to do."

"Lulu Belle, what have you gotten yourself into now," he whispered, clenching the part in his hand. He focused on the comlink in his ear. "Bulldog!" He growled in a low, not completely steady voice. "Tell me you have Skeeter with you."

* * *

Skeeter leaned back and looked at the wall with a sad smile. She and Manny, her new temporary co-pilot, were on their way back to Sallas after dropping off her cargo on Newport. She had decided before the trip that it was time to be honest with her dad and tell him that she wasn't a very good freighter captain. What she really wanted to do was focus on her art.

She and Bulldog had talked well into the night shortly after Krac had left. She didn't know why she thought it would be so hard to tell him or why she feared he would be disappointed. A small smile curved her lips as she thought back to their conversation.

* * *

"Why didn't you tell me you knew all along?" She had asked as she sat snuggled up on the couch in his office.

"You have been decorating our home since you arrived with pictures and things you have made," Bulldog had responded with a smile. "I know because I have every single one you have created. I have always been very proud of your talent. I just wanted you to know where you would be happiest."

"So, you aren't disappointed if I focus on my art? I already have several pieces in some of the galleries on Newport, Gallus and even Pryus."

Of course, he had been thrilled. It was only later as she lay sleepless in her bed that felt empty without Krac's warm body against hers, that she laughed at herself for being so stupid. It was ridiculous to think that her dad didn't know about her gallery showings. He knew everything about everything. Still, having his support and acceptance meant the world to her.

* * *

That this was her last trip on the *Lulu Belle* made the time even more bittersweet as she stared at her newest painting. She sank down into the chair and stared at the wall in Froget's old cabin. The painting of him was so real, she felt like she could reach out and touch him. A single tear coursed down her face as she remembered the first morning after he had started as her co-pilot. He had come up to the bridge in a very grumpy mood. When she asked him what was wrong, he had exploded, saying he hadn't slept all night because he kept trying to eat the damn red and black bugs that were all over his walls.

"My tongue is so sore I can barely talk straight," he had mumbled.

She wiped at the second tear that fell and chuckled. He hadn't been lying. His tongue had hung out of the side of his mouth for almost two weeks before he stopped trying to eat them.

Now, he sat in the middle of a small field. The sun was shining down on him and dozens of the little red and black bugs snuggled up close to him as he smiled back at her.

"Thank you, my dear, dear friend," Skeeter whispered, sadly. "I'll never forget you."

"Skeeter," Manny's voice called from the doorway.

Skeeter glanced over and smiled at the elderly Chibear. He wasn't much taller than Froget but instead of having smooth skin, he was covered in a soft gray fur. Manny had worked for her dad for years as a freighter pilot before retiring to care for the gardens at their home. Bulldog insisted that if she was going to finish her delivery she needed to have an experienced co-pilot. Manny agreed to go with her as it gave him a chance to see his daughter and her mate who owned a shop on Newport.

"Yes, Manny?" She said, standing and wiping at her damp cheeks.

"There is something strange going on with your navigation system," he said with a frown. "Strange star charts keep popping up and there are symbols I've never seen before. I don't recognize any of them. I ran a diagnostic to see if it was defective, but everything came back showing it was working properly."

Skeeter sighed. This was a part of being a freighter captain that she wasn't going to miss at all. She bent and gathered up her paint and brushes. She would need to clean them before she could take a look at what Manny was talking about.

"Are we still heading for Sallas?" She asked as she stepped out into the corridor. "Is the malfunction causing a problem?"

"Yes, we are still on course for Sallas. It isn't so much a malfunction. It is just I've never in all my eighty years as a pilot seen the star systems it is showing and the translators can't decipher the code," Manny complained, walking slowly beside her toward the galley. "I've been to just about every known star system at least once. These are some I've never even heard of."

"I'll have daddy's maintenance crew take a look at it when we get back to Sallas," Skeeter said with a shrugged. "This is a replacement module I picked up.

Our old one was fried. I found this one on Pryus and Frog... Froget was able to modify it so it would work."

Manny nodded before jumping when an alarm suddenly sounded. Skeeter froze for a moment, trying to remember what Krac had told her about the alarms. This one was different from the one that sounded when she hit something. A moment later, the alarm stopped. She quickly laid the brushes she had cleaned on the towel next to the sink before grabbing another one to dry her hands.

"Which alarm was that for?" She asked, looking down at Manny in confusion. "The one that sounds when I hit something is a lot louder and doesn't stop."

Manny's chubby face wrinkled into a concerned frown. "It is the security. It would only go off if there was a breach in one of the outer access doors. There must be a short in it otherwise the defense system would have kicked in and the security alarms would have stayed on and sealed the doors after thirty seconds. I'll take a look at it," he said with a shake of his head. "Your father should have purchased you a newer model freighter. This one is falling apart."

Skeeter bit back the giggle at his disgusted look. She didn't want to confess that her dad had purchased her a newer freighter, three in fact. She was hopeless with all the newer technology on them and he had finally given up and settled for a simpler model.

"Krac was working on both the defense and security systems," she finally admitted. "Neither were working before. I guess they broke again."

"Your systems are working properly," a new voice said coolly. "I bypassed them."

Skeeter squeaked in surprise while Manny emitted a low growl and moved to stand protectively in front of her. Her lips parted in surprise as she gazed at the huge male standing in the doorway to the galley pointing a laser pistol at them.

He was as tall as Krac and just as distinctive with his silver/gray skin and almost black eyes. He looked a little younger than Krac though and wore his hair longer. He was dressed all in black and another pistol hung from his waist.

Skeeter's eyes jerked back to his when he snapped out a warning to Manny to not move. Her hands dropped to her old friend's shoulders and she held him back against her. She would not let another die for her again.

"Manny, it's okay," she whispered, watching the male in the doorway warily. "He's just like Krac."

The male in the doorway stiffened at her softly spoken words. His eyes flashed with barely restrained rage before he concealed the emotion behind a mask of calm. He stepped into the room, his eyes sweeping the area carefully before settling back on them.

"Where is the other male like me?" He asked sharply.

Skeeter tilted her head and smiled nervously at the male. Even though he was holding a pistol on them, he reminded her too much of Krac to be afraid. Besides, while he exuded an air of danger, there was also an air of desperation that pulled at her.

"He's not here. I think he might be looking for you," she said with a small, nervous smile as she stepped around Manny. "You know, we aren't going to hurt you. You can put your weapon down."

"Skeeter!" Manny hissed. "What do you think you are doing?"

Skeeter rolled her eyes. "This is Manny. He is my friend. I don't want you to hurt him." She bit her lip as she remembered poor Froget. "Why are you looking for Krac? You aren't going to hurt him, are you? I have to tell you, I won't let that happen. I happen to love the big guy and I'm very protective of those I love."

* * *

Section L stared at the strange female looking back at him in defiance. She was now standing in front of the small furry creature with her hands on her hips. She had green and yellow paint across one cheek. It looked as if she had forgotten she was painting and brushed her fingers along it. There were additional splatters of paint on her arms and clothing. Her dark red hair was piled on top of her head with strands falling loosely from the clasp holding it. Even that had not been spared as color was mixed in with it as well.

She was one of the most bizarre humans that he had encountered. Only one other female had ever looked at him with that same look of defiance. He slammed the door on the image that flowed into his mind along with the pain it brought with it. He was here on a mission.

"I hope he is capable of having feelings for you as well," Section L said with a cold, menacing smile as he fired the laser pistol twice.

He watched as the red-haired woman's eyes briefly widened before she collapsed. His second shot took out the smaller male. He sheathed the pistol before walking over to the unusual pair. Kneeling, he felt each of their throats before picking up the smaller male and tossing him over his shoulder.

Now, it was time to see if the male the female cared about felt the same way. He suspected from the female's reaction to him that the male would not only come for her, he would be willing do anything to keep her safe. He would use that against the male when he came.

Section L lowered the small male into the seat of the escape pod and strapped him in. Ducking his head, he stepped out of the small vessel and sealed it. He connected to the controls and pre-set a course back toward Newport. He set a delay on the emergency transmission to go off in two hours. This would give him time to do what he needed to do before any vessels in the transport lanes picked up the distress call and came to pick the male up.

He watched as the pod shot out of the narrow tube into space before the outer door closed again. With a satisfied smile, he turned and headed back to the galley. Now it was time to take care of the female.

Chapter 27

"I don't give a damn what you want," Bulldog growled. "I have a location lock on the *Lulu Belle*. I'll be there in seven hours."

"I will be there in three," Krac replied coldly. "The escape pod was picked up an hour ago. Skeeter's co-pilot was the only one aboard. He was unconscious."

"I've been trying to hail the *Lulu Belle* since you notified me," Bulldog admitted. "There has been no response."

"Perhaps it is not you that they want to talk to," Krac growled in a low voice filled with rage.

"I knew I should have killed your ass," Bulldog retorted. "If anything happens to my daughter, I'm going to gut you slowly for bringing her into your fight."

Krac drew in a deep, calming breath before releasing it. If he wanted to get Skeeter out of this alive, he needed to push the overwhelming feelings threatening to drown him away. He needed to think logically, clearly, if he wanted to defeat the one or ones responsible for taking over the *Lulu Belle* and kidnapping her.

He glanced down at the frozen image on the vidcom on the console in front of him. The male staring back at him had made sure he was the only one who received the coded message. It was in a language known only to a very few. A language not taught, but passed down through the genetic coding of their ancestors.

I have something that you want. You have something that I want. Lulu Belle.

The last two words sent a sickening wave through him. The thought of Skeeter's gentle soul being held by another of his kind, a monster capable of killing her without remorse and with extreme cruelty, chilled him. He would kill the bastard.

"There is something else going on," Krac replied instead. "Skeeter found something besides Violet when she went to the Parts shop on Pryus."

"What?" Bulldog snapped.

"Her navigation system wasn't working correctly. I found the original navigation module from the *Lulu Belle* on a shelf in the shop. I suspect she found a replacement while she was there. I noticed that Froget had been working on it, but I was focused on repairing the other systems that weren't working and did not complete a diagnostic on it," he analyzed.

"That damn girl can get in trouble without even trying," Bulldog finally said in a gruff voice. "I guarantee she didn't know what in the hell she was grabbing. The girl is an okay pilot, but she doesn't know anything about repairs."

"Then why in the hell did you let her pilot a freighter?" Krac growled. "I should be the one gutting you just for that!"

"Have you ever seen her with tears in her eyes?" Bulldog replied, his voice softening. "She was determined to find something that she could do to make me proud of her. She just didn't have a clue that I've been proud of her from the moment she crawled out from under the storage unit, snapping and growling at me before she wound her tiny arms around my heart. We talked while you were gone. She finally admitted she wants to focus on her art. I expect you to support her desire as well."

Krac heard the emotion in the huge Triterian's voice. It was strange to believe that a creature as fierce, deadly and cold-blooded as Bulldog could have feelings like that. A shaft of pain swept through him when he realized he could have been describing himself. He suddenly felt very vulnerable.

"Why do you call her Skeeter?" He asked in a husky voice.

Bulldog's soft chuckle echoed through the communications console. "She was a little bitty thing, all wild red hair and long skinny arms and legs. I bought Tila from one of the mining facilities that we stopped at shortly after finding her. Tila had spent time on Earth when she was younger, so she was familiar with human offspring. Lulu Belle was always getting into everything and curious. She annoyed the hell out of my crew, but no one but Tila or I could pick her up and move her without her snapping and biting them. Tila said Lulu Belle reminded her of the small creatures back on Earth known as mosquitoes. She said they were small and annoying and had a tendency to draw blood. The region where she lived at she said they were often referred to as skeeters. One of the crew heard Tila and soon everyone on board my ship was calling Lulu Belle that. Lulu Belle heard it and liked it so much, she wouldn't answer unless you called her by that name."

Krac felt his chest tighten as he thought about Skeeter as the frightened little girl that she had been. The fact that she had survived was a miracle from the records he had tapped into while at Bulldog's compound. What was even more of a miracle was that someone as beautiful as her could love a creature such as him.

"I'm approaching the *Lulu Belle* now," Krac responded. "I will contact you once I have taken control of it."

"Find and protect my daughter and kill the bastards," Bulldog replied. "If you don't, I will."

* * *

Krac felt the weak connection the moment he stepped aboard the freighter. The faint brush of awareness of the other male. He had no doubt the other male felt it as well. He skimmed his palm over the panel near the doorway. In seconds, he knew that the programming for the defense and security system had been changed. He jerked his hand back when a slight surge of power sent a jolt through his hand.

"Smart bastard," Krac muttered under his breath as he blocked the warning when he tried to access the PLT he had reactivated. Without it, he would have to search for where not only the male was, but Skeeter. "Where is she?"

"She is secure," a voice echoed across the wide cargo bay. "I'm impressed. I did not expect you for several more hours."

Krac watched as a tall male stepped out of the shadows. He immediately did a scan. Two weapons, laser pistols, were at the male's waist. Their build and muscle density were approximately the same. This model was younger than him. There was the possibility of a difference in combat experience, but that was no guarantee.

"Where is she?" Krac asked, sliding the curved blades he liked to use into his hands. "Did you harm her?"

"You have feelings for her? She said she loved you," the male remarked with a cool smile. "You have lost the ability to hide your emotions. That makes you vulnerable."

Krac felt rage build inside at the male's mocking tone. He rotated his wrists and rolled his shoulders. He would cut the bastard's head from his shoulders.

"It also makes you more dangerous," the male added as he paused about three meters from him. "It also gives you a reason to fight against what is to come."

Krac paused at the softly spoken words. His eyes narrowed on the male who stood watching him with cool, calm eyes. He winced when he felt the mild pressure again before stiffening in shock.

Can you hear me?

What the....

Good. We are linked.

"What the fuck are you doing?" Krac snarled as the voice faded from his head.

"I was not sure it would work. If we are to be successful, it is imperative that we have every advantage possible. I am... Seal," the male replied. "The Leader knows me as Section L."

Krac remained wary as the male took another cautious step toward him. The cool mask on the male's face changed as anger flashed through his eyes at the mention of The Leader before being replaced again. He felt the pressure in his mind again, but this time was able to block it.

"Where is the female?" He demanded.

"She is resting in her cabin. I stunned her, but there is no permanent damage," Seal responded quietly.

"What do you want?" Krac asked. "You said the Leader knows you as Section L. Who is the Leader?"

Seal sighed in frustration, glaring down at the floor before he looked back at Krac. Frustration was clearly evident on his face as he returned Krac's steady gaze. So was the anger that darkened his eyes to midnight.

"I don't know," Seal admitted. "If I did I would have killed him long ago. The only contact I have is through a special comlink."

"Yet you are here because the Leader sent you," Krac remarked, moving slightly closer.

"Yes," Seal responded shortly. "Your female took a navigational module that the Leader wants. I am to terminate her, and you if given the opportunity, and return with it immediately."

"I'll show you termination," another dark voice growled.

Krac and Seal turned at the same time as Bulldog moved silently out of the shadows. The smooth scales covering his face and neck a brilliant dark red and cold fury blazing from his eyes. He fired two of the six laser pistols in his hands.

Seal's body lifted off the ground as the powerful double blasts hit him in the chest. Krac yelled out as the younger Allbreed flew through the air, landing almost five meters away. He sheathed the blades and raced forward.

"Damn it, Bulldog. He has information that could help the Confederation and the Earth councils," Krac bit out as he bent of the still figure of the male. "I thought you said you were seven hours out."

"I lied. The bastard was talking about terminating my daughter," Bulldog snorted. "If he isn't dead, I'll rip his guts out to make sure of it."

Krac ignored the furious Triterian, instead focusing on the damage to the male's chest. Even as he ripped open the black material covering Seal's shredded chest, he could see the male's tissue reforming and sealing. Relief washed through him even as he wondered what in the hell was going to happen next.

"You can't rip his guts out until we know what is going on," Krac replied, glancing up where Bulldog stood over his shoulder. "If he has harmed or tries to harm Skeeter, I'll be the one to rip his guts out."

"I would prefer to keep them, if you don't mind," a faint, hoarse voice muttered. "This is… this is bigger than you think."

Krac's face turned grim as the male shut down his system to preserve the blood loss as his body healed itself. He gripped the male's arms and rose. With a nod of his head, he glared at Bulldog.

"Grab his feet. We'll take him to medical," he snapped. "I need to find Skeeter. He said she was resting in her cabin."

Bulldog grunted as he grabbed Seal's legs with his two lower hands. "She better be or I'll start breaking bones faster than he can heal them."

Chapter 28

Krac's fingers shook as he gently traced the delicate outline of Skeeter's cheek. Her hair was spread wildly out over the soft gray pillow. A tender smile curved his lips at the dried paint on her.

"She is well?" Bulldog's gruff voice asked from the doorway.

"Yes, just sedated," Krac responded, continuing to tenderly caress her. "She is beautiful."

"She is the sun. She gives life to the world around her," Bulldog murmured. "I will watch over the other male. If I'm lucky, he'll try to attack me and I can watch him try to heal himself again."

Krac shook his head and bit back an amused chuckle. "How did you manage to maim and dismember with Skeeter around? She faints at the sight of blood."

"I know," Bulldog muttered, turning to leave. "I had to cut back a lot until she left home. At the rate she was going through co-pilots, I made up for it though."

Krac glanced over his shoulder at Bulldog who had paused to study him. "Thank you for that, especially for the one called Terry."

Bulldog's face creased in a huge smile and his eyes twinkled with a devilish sparkle. "That one was done with extreme pleasure. That bastard would have never be able to use another man's daughter again. I made sure of that… before I killed him."

"I thought he was at Cramoore," Krac said in surprise.

"He had an accident on the way there," Bulldog smirked. "A very unpleasant one. I'd better go. I have no idea how fast that bastard can heal himself."

Krac nodded, turning back around to gaze down at Skeeter. Her lips were parted now and she was snoring lightly. His throat tightened as he released the fear he had buried when he discovered she was in danger.

He carefully scooted her over and climbed onto the bed so he could lie down next to her. The moment he stretched out, she released a soft sigh and rolled over. He slid his arm under her and pulled her closer, wincing slightly when her knee connected with his groin before she settled back down.

"I love you, Lulu Belle," he whispered as he stroked her. "I love you so much it frightens me to think of something happening to you."

He sighed and chuckled when she responded with a soft snore in his ear. He pressed a kiss to her forehead and stared up at the twinkling lights. His mind running over all the information he had gathered and the strange comments of the male called Seal. The one that concerned him the most was the male's last statement.

This is… this is bigger than you think.

A shiver of unease ran through him. He hoped Bulldog refrained from his threats of gutting the male. He had a feeling things were about to go to hell fast.

* * *

Two hours later, he, Bulldog and a weak, but mostly healed, Seal sat in the galley of the *Lulu Belle*.

Seal glared moodily at Bulldog who glared right back. Krac felt like he was going to have to send them both to the corner to cool off if they didn't stop soon.

He shifted and silently cursed as he adjusted his semi-hard cock. It would appear, once relief that Skeeter was safe swept through him, another emotion came with it; the need to claim her again and reassure himself that she was his. It didn't help that she spread out over him and her hand had wrapped around him in her sleep.

"How much of the damn sedative did you give her?" Krac asked suddenly. "She is still asleep."

"Not much," Seal mumbled. "I think she was tired before I shot her. She had dark circles under her eyes. Ouch! Why did you do that? Isn't blasting my chest to pieces enough torture?" Seal glared at Bulldog as he rubbed his arm where the Triterian punched him.

"For shooting my daughter," Bulldog said stubbornly.

"I stunned her! I didn't blast her chest open. And she obviously needed the rest if she is still asleep," Seal snapped back.

Krac fought the urge to shoot both of the males sitting across from him. If it wasn't that so much depended on learning what Seal knew and Skeeter would never forgive him for killing her father, he would have already done it. Anything to be alone with her. He was about to threaten them both when a horrendous yell exploded from the doorway.

He started to rise before falling backwards in his seat. He stared at the figure in the doorway with a look of stunned horror that gradually turned to disbelief before turning to a bizarre fascination.

"What the hell...?" Seal muttered, looking in horror at the wild red hair, painted face and bugged eyes of the female. "I did not do that to her. You can't blame this on me."

Krac's lips twitched when she bent and slapped her thighs and stuck her tongue out as far as she could. She had dark lines drawn on her face and her hair stood out like wild flames silhouetting her face. She started chanting in a strange language as she moved. Her eyes bulged and she moved back and forth, her arms stiff and her fists clenched around a long wooden pole. Unease washed through him as she moved closer. A faint memory tickling him as she continued her bizarre dance. The memory hit him a moment before she did. The end of the wooden pole connected with his jaw before the breath hissed out of him when she swung forward.

He fell backwards out of his chair and hit the floor at the same time as she made another loud screech. He winced when the end of the pole connected with Seal's crotch as he was rising out of his seat before it came up and caught him under the jaw, knocking him back against the wall.

Krac almost felt sorry for the younger male as he turned a very pale silver and slid down the floor clutching his groin while a thin stream of blood ran down his chin. He ducked and rolled when the pole flashed past his head again. This time, he was able to grab the slender leg as it stomped down next to him.

He reached up and grabbed the waistband of Skeeter's pants and yanked her off-balance.

His arms caught her as she fell and he rolled, pinning her under him. He quickly grabbed her flailing arms and laid one of his thick thighs over her legs to prevent her from kneeing him. It took several long seconds before the wild look cleared from her eyes. He watched as she blinked rapidly before relaxing back against the floor.

"Hi. I missed you," she said breathlessly.

"I can tell," he chuckled, looking down at her with a critical eye. "What in the hell was that and what have you done to your face?"

"I was doing a Haka War Dance. I thought I could scare the other guy away. It was used by the Maori on old Earth to intimidate their enemy," she explained, tilting her head to look at where the other male sat against the wall with his eyes closed. "See, it worked!"

A low chuckle started behind them and drew her attention. Her eyes widened and a huge smile spread across her face as a very familiar red-skinned face appeared over Krac's left shoulder. The amused face of her father stared down at her.

"Hi daddy," Skeeter said. "I'm getting better at the maiming."

A low moan from the wall drew her attention again. This time her eyes focused on his face. Her lips parted before her eyes rolled back in her head as the male smeared the blood running from his mouth across his jaw in disgust.

Bulldog shook his head in amusement. "Yes, my sunshine. You have mastered the maiming but you still can't handle the blood."

Krac sighed as he slowly released Skeeter's limp arms. He rose up, picking her up as he did. He glanced first at her before looking at where Seal still sat on the floor.

"She will be out for at least twenty minutes," he said. "When she wakes, you have a lot of explaining to do."

"Will she do this every time she wakes up?" Seal asked, slowly rising off the floor. "I thought she was human. Her DNA scan said she was."

"She is," Krac retorted. "Get cleaned up. She faints at the sight of blood."

Seal rubbed the front of his pants gingerly before glaring at Bulldog who had returned to his seat at the table and was watching him with amusement. He bent and picked up the two fallen chairs before walking over to the galley sink and washing his mouth out.

He glared at Bulldog again as he sank painfully down into the chair. There were some pain sensors in his body that even he had trouble turning off. He sent a command for the nanobots in his body to repair the bruised tissue. It was taking longer since he was still trying to repair the damage from earlier.

"Can you tell me what in the hell just happened?" He asked, pulling the cup of liquor Bulldog had pushed toward him closer. "Is she always like that?"

"Of course," Bulldog replied with a proud smile. "She is my daughter."

"Great. This mission is totally fucked," Seal muttered, closing his eyes and lowering his head as fatigue from the repairs to his body and his mission pulled on him. "Totally, absolutely fucked."

Chapter 29

"So you are saying you believe there is information on the navigation module that Skeeter took from the part's shop on Pryus that could possibly destroy the Confederation," Krac said.

"I believe so," Seal said. "I was sent to retrieve it at all cost. The Leader of the New Order himself instructed me to return with it to Earth. I am to give it directly to him. I plan on killing him when I do," he added coldly.

"Why do you want to kill the Leader?" Krac asked skeptically. "You have been working for him."

Seal looked away before turning back to stare at Krac with a blank face. "My reasons are my own. The Leader believes he still has control of me. What he doesn't know is that I was able to disable the implant the scientist embedded in my brain."

"How?" Bulldog asked, leaning forward. "It stands to reason that the scientists would have created a precaution against you being able to do that."

Seal's lips tightened into a straight line. "I had help. It has been disabled. I have to return with the module, but I want to know what is on it first."

"I know," Skeeter spoke up excitedly.

Three pairs of eyes turned to her in surprise. "Froget mentioned it and Manny did too. I was going to get daddy's maintenance crew to take a look at it."

"What is on it?" Krac asked, reaching for her hand as it fluttered.

"Star charts. Ones that Manny has never seen. He said it was strange as he had never seen any of them in the eighty years he was a freighter captain. He said there were strange symbols, possibly a language that the translator couldn't translate."

I don't like this.

Krac's head jerked toward Seal who was staring at him silently. He gave a slight nod to his head to show he heard him. His lips tightened at the other male's shared thoughts.

"I think it best if Seal and I take a look at the module. Bulldog, we may need to take the module out of your starship and modify it for the *Lulu Belle* so we can get it back to Sallas. Can you bring it up to the bridge?" Krac asked.

Bulldog's eyes glittered with suspicion, but he nodded. "Of course."

"Skeeter," Krac started to say.

"Is going to the bridge to see what you two discover," she finished for him. "Daddy has tried the distraction thing too many times. I figured it out a long time ago."

Bulldog sighed in relief. "Good enough for me. I'll get the module after we find out what is going on."

Krac bit back a curse while Seal looked at him with a cynical smirk. "This whole mission hasn't gone the way I planned so who am I to argue. Besides, your female might go all Maori on my ass again if I tell her no."

"Let's find out what is on the module," Krac said in exasperation.

* * *

Can you understand this?

Krac gave a sharp nod. He could understand it and what he was seeing wasn't good. His eyes scanned the symbols, the translation running through his mind as if he had spoken the language every day of his life. What concerned him was this was the first time he had ever seen it.

Ordinances, positions, directives.

This is a plan for a full assault. There are hundreds of motherships. If they all came at the same time, it would overwhelm the Confederations defenses. Even the combined forces of all the planets would not be enough to defeat the number of fighters held in half that many ships.

The council needs to know.

"Okay, what is going on? You two are doing the frown and stare thing again," Skeeter said in exasperation. "Daddy, do you recognize any of this?"

Bulldog was silent for several long moments. His eyes locked on the star charts showing on the console. He trembled when he felt Skeeter's slender hand slide into one of his hands.

"Yes," Bulldog said hoarsely. "I've seen it. I've been to it. A long time ago. A very, very long time ago."

Both Krac and Seal focused on Bulldog's face. "How? What happened?"

Bulldog sighed and tore his gaze from the screen to look at the two males. "I'm older than you think. The Triterians can live for hundreds of years. All Triterians are required to serve fifty years in the military. I was part of an elite scouting team. Our job was to go where no others could or wanted to go. During my tenth year, we were at war with the Octoply. They had attacked several of the outer colonies hoping to take over some of the most profitable mining operations that we were running. It took a while before we figured out the damn creatures could regrow their limbs if we blew them off. Anyway, I watched a squadron of them come out of nowhere but they weren't alone. Other fighters, unlike anything I had ever seen, were following them. It was a short fight. The coordination of the other squadron was unbelievable. I had never seen anything like it. It was as if they acted as one. What shocked me was when they turned and disappeared just as quickly as they appeared."

"What did you do?" Seal asked.

"I followed them. There is an anomaly in that section, almost like a rip in space. There was no light, nothing. When my fighter went through, it was as if time and space had folded in on itself. The next thing I knew, I was in a star system that I had never seen. None of the readings made sense. I began recording the information. It was what I was trained to do. I was into my second day when a large signal lit up my sensors. Something told me I needed to go silent. The scout fighters were designed with a special metal that helps hide our presence. That is probably the only thing that saved my hide," Bulldog reflected in a solemn voice.

"What did you see?" Skeeter asked, squeezing her dad's hand again when it trembled.

"I saw a planet built of metal and thousands of warships unlike anything I had seen before in different phases of construction. I withdrew and returned to my squadron. I reported my findings, but nothing was ever done as far as I could tell and I never saw those fighters again until..." His voice faded as he stared at Krac. "...until the attacks on the mining facilities a couple years ago. I heard about the Earth woman named Jones and the rumors about her. I was curious and did some research of my own. The Earth has done a good job with maintaining their archives of the events of the attack on their planet. What I saw was the same ships, only larger and more of them."

"You didn't perchance keep a copy of the information you recorded, including where this anomaly is, would you?" Krac asked in a quiet voice.

Bulldog's lips curved up in a grim smile. "Of course, I did. Not only do I have both, I have something a little better," he responded.

"What?" Seal asked, sitting up straight at the sound of satisfaction in Bulldog's voice.

"I visited that area on my own once more after I got out of the military. I caught one of the little bastards alone. They aren't as good a fighter one-on-one. I killed the bastard and brought his fighter home. Where do you think I got some of the technology I've developed over the years?" Bulldog said. "It has made me a very rich man."

* * *

Several hours later, Skeeter waited for Krac and her father to return to the bridge. They had contacted Kordon Jefe and Bran Markus, the Zion Grand Admiral. Seal was resistant at first to others knowing about him and their findings, but Krac assured him that the men could be trusted to keep the information to themselves until additional information was known.

"Kordon's mate, Gracie, understands the language as well as we do. She has also had direct contact with them. This may be why the leader wants her. To translate the information," Krac explained quietly. "There is no way for the Leader to know that you and I can also understand it. While the Confederation scientists are learning, they still have a long way to go before they can understand it to the extent that Gracie can."

"This is serious, Krac," Gracie had said. "From the little I've been able to read, there are embedded directives within the star charts. The directives appear to be instructions for mapping our planet location and testing resistance. The first Mothership was deployed to scout the area, determine the defense capabilities of the region and report usable resources. We destroyed it before it could return with the information."

"Why would the Leader of the New Order want this information?" Kordon asked, looking suspiciously at Seal.

"Maybe they want it for the same reason daddy did," Skeeter said.

A loud curse escaped Kordon as he turned his cold gaze on Bulldog. "The shields you developed! I recognize the similarities now."

Bulldog shrugged. "A little modification and I was able to make a decent profit off of it."

"Or maybe something more," Seal interrupted quietly. His fists clenched until his knuckles shown white.

"Like what?" Bran demanded.

"An implant was embedded inside me," Seal spoke slowly, remembering the pain and overwhelming feeling of being out of control of his own body. "I was taken from the research facilities the day before it was raided. I don't remember much as I was heavily sedated. I do remember when they implanted the device inside my skull. I was unable to shut down the pain sensors. Afterwards... afterwards, it was as if I had lost all control of my body and at times, my mind. Commands were sent and there was nothing I could do to resist. If I tried... if I tried the pain was overwhelming."

"The Alluthans are controlled by a hive mentality," Gracie reflected softly. "If you control the leader, you control the workers."

"Or soldiers in this case," Bran murmured.

"You have a massive army at your beck and call," Kordon finished. "One that outnumbers the Confederation a thousand to one."

"You said you were able to disable the implant," Skeeter reminded Seal. "Couldn't it just be disabled if this Leader tries to use it?"

"That could be just as devastating," Bulldog reminded her. "Then you have the leader of the Alluthans back in control of its massive fleet in Confederation space."

"I wasn't the one who was able to disable it. There is another person who knows how to disable the implant. The one who designed it," Seal commented. "The Leader... tried to kill the researcher after stealing the design."

"Who?" Kordon demanded.

"Morgan Miller. Anastasia Miller's younger sister. If I do not return with the module, he will kill her," Seal replied quietly.

"Krac, contact Roarrk and Anastasia. Tell them to get Morgan somewhere safe. I don't care if they have to bury her ass under a mountain," Kordon ordered.

"No!" Seal interrupted, sitting forward. "The Leader was able to get inside to Morgan. Whoever it is can move freely among the council. I just don't know who the hell it is. If anyone tries to move Morgan, including her sister, she'll be murdered. I... I have to return. When I do, I'll either kill the bastard when we meet for the exchange or I'll get her out. Any sudden changes and the Leader will know."

"You can't give them the information," Gracie protested.

"No, I can't," Seal agreed. "But, I can give the Leader false information. He still thinks I am under his control. It will buy time to get Morgan out safely and time to find out what in the hell the Alluthans are planning."

"How can we do that? We would need to travel to their star system, board one of the motherships and connect to it, all without being caught," Bran said skeptically.

"You would need a way to link with them to really know what is going on," Gracie added, biting her lip.

"We would need an Alluthan to do that," Kordon responded, looking at Krac and Seal.

"Or one of us," Krac reflected quietly.

Chapter 30

Skeeter looked up at her father and nodded before her eyes moved to Krac who stood staring at her with a quiet hunger in his eyes. She rose and moved toward him instinctively, knowing he needed to hold her as much as she needed to hold him. She glanced at her father who nodded his head in understanding.

"Thank you, daddy," she whispered, clutching Krac's hand in hers.

"He makes you happy, Lulu Belle," Bulldog murmured, brushing her red hair back from her face. "That is all I've ever wanted."

"I love you," she said with a tender smile and rose up onto her toes and brushed a kiss along his cheek.

Bulldog sighed as he watched Krac put a protective arm around his daughter's waist. He sat down in the captain's seat and pulled up the star charts again. As he studied them he thought of the huge male who had claimed his little girl.

"If I had to choose someone who could protect her from what is to come, I couldn't have chosen any better," he murmured to himself. "I love you, baby girl. I promised to always protect you. Now you have someone who might be able to do a better job than even me."

* * *

Krac sealed the door behind him as they stepped into Skeeter's cabin. They were heading back to Sallas but it would be a short stay. They would be leaving the *Lulu Belle* behind and traveling on to Paulus, the capital of the Confederation, shortly after that.

"What is going to happen?" She asked quietly, her fingers slowly undoing the buttons of his shirt.

"A mission to the Alluthan star system more than likely," he answered her, briefly closing his eyes as her fingers caressed his shoulders as she pushed his shirt off. "At worse, war."

"You are going to have to go on the mission, aren't you?" She asked in a trembling voice as her hands rubbed over his chest.

"Probably, along with Seal and the other two Allbreeds if he can find them. It makes the most sense," he said heavily. "Perhaps this is the reason we were created."

Skeeter heard the hesitation in his voice, the doubt and a touch of self-loathing. She gently cupped his face, forcing him to look at her. Reaching up on her toes, she brushed a kiss across his lips tenderly before deepening it when he groaned.

Her arms wrapped around his neck as he lifted her up in his arms and carefully laid her down on the soft covers of her bed. She sighed when he pulled back far enough to look down at her. His fingers gently kneaded her hips as he stared into her eyes as if trying to decide whether she would accept what he was about to tell her.

"I was not born, Lulu Belle. I was created in a lab. A mutation of human and Alluthan DNA. Even the scientists who created us thought of us as monsters. They were trying to perfect what the Alluthans had started. They wanted the ultimate weapon, one that could regenerate itself and heal its wounds. They wanted a cold, emotionless killing machine," he whispered.

"And they made you," she said with a tender smile. She raised her left hand and ran her fingers along his face. "They made a wonderful man who lit a fire inside me that I've never felt before. They made a man who can protect those of us who can't what is to come without your help. They made..."

"A monster! Didn't you hear what I said?" He asked harshly. He wanted – needed - her to understand that if she was with him, others wouldn't see what she saw. "I am a monster."

"Then they were blind," she replied. "A monster is someone like Harden. He killed Frog because he enjoyed it. A monster is like the Leader of the New Order and his followers who would destroy millions of lives and worlds for power. That is what a monster is. You, you are none of those things. I love you, Krac. I love the man inside here," she whispered, touching her hand over his heart. "I love the man who would fight to protect a little girl from the monsters of the world. I love the man who would stand up to a full-grown Triterian and tell him he was sleeping wherever his daughter was sleeping. I love a man who would fight for what he believes in. You are that man."

Krac could see the sincerity in Skeeter's eyes as she stared into his. Her heart shone in them as she talked of who she saw. He blinked as an unfamiliar burning stung them. He lowered his head, burying it in her shoulder and pressed a hot kiss to the side of her neck.

"I love you, Lulu Belle," he whispered in a voice thick with emotion. "I don't know what the future holds for any of us, but I want mine to have you in it forever."

"Krac," she murmured. "I hurt."

His warm breath caressed her neck as he released a chuckle. She ran her hands along the smooth skin of his back and rotated her hips. A small knowing smile lit up her face when she felt his response.

"I know how to make it stop," he chuckled again.

"I was hoping you would say that," she breathed, before gasping as he sat back and ripped her shirt open. "You know, I'm not going to have any clothes left."

"Good," he growled. "I like you without them on."

Skeeter moaned as his hands moved up to her breasts, cupping them while his forefingers and thumbs pinched the taut nipples. It was becoming a familiar argument with them. One that she hoped would continue for many, many decades as he quickly took care of the rest of her clothes.

To be continued: Roarrk's Revenge

If you loved this story by me (S. E. Smith) please leave a review (just keep swiping, LOL). You can also take a look at additional books and sign up for my newsletter at http://sesmithfl.com to hear about my latest releases or keep in touch using the following links:

Website: http://sesmithfl.com
Newsletter: http://sesmithfl.com/?s=newsletter
Facebook: https://www.facebook.com/se.smith.5
Twitter: https://twitter.com/sesmithfl
Pinterest: http://www.pinterest.com/sesmithfl/
Blog: http://sesmithfl.com/blog/
Forum: http://www.sesmithromance.com/forum/

Additional Books by S. E. Smith

Paranormal and Science Fiction short stories and novellas

For the Love of Tia (Dragon Lords of Valdier Book 4.1)

A Dragonlings' Easter (Dragonlings of Valdier Book 1)

A Warrior's Heart (Marastin Dow Warriors Book 1.1)

Rescuing Mattie (Lords of Kassis: Book 3.1)

Science Fiction/Paranormal Novels

Cosmos' Gateway Series

Tink's Neverland (Cosmo's Gateway: Book 1)

Hannah's Warrior (Cosmos' Gateway: Book 2)

Tansy's Titan (Cosmos' Gateway: Book 3)

Cosmos' Promise (Cosmos' Gateway: Book 4)

Curizan Warrior

Ha'ven's Song (Curizan Warrior: Book 1)

Dragon Lords of Valdier

Abducting Abby (Dragon Lords of Valdier: Book 1)

Capturing Cara (Dragon Lords of Valdier: Book 2)

Tracking Trisha (Dragon Lords of Valdier: Book 3)
Ambushing Ariel (Dragon Lords of Valdier: Book 4)
Cornering Carmen (Dragon Lords of Valdier: Book 5)
Paul's Pursuit (Dragon Lords of Valdier: Book 6)
Twin Dragons (Dragon Lords of Valdier: Book 7)
Lords of Kassis Series
River's Run (Lords of Kassis: Book 1)
Star's Storm (Lords of Kassis: Book 2)
Jo's Journey (Lords of Kassis: Book 3)
Magic, New Mexico Series
Touch of Frost (Magic, New Mexico Book 1)
Sarafin Warriors
Choosing Riley (Sarafin Warriors: Book 1)
The Alliance Series
Hunter's Claim (The Alliance: Book 1)
Razor's Traitorous Heart (The Alliance: Book 2)
Zion Warriors Series
Gracie's Touch (Zion Warriors: Book 1)
Krac's Firebrand (Zion Warriors: Book 2)
Paranormal and Time Travel Novels
Spirit Pass Series
Indiana Wild (Spirit Pass: Book 1)
Heaven Sent Series
Lily's Cowboys (Heaven Sent: Book 1)
Touching Rune (Heaven Sent: Book 2)
Excerpts of S. E. Smith Books
If you would like to read more S. E. Smith stories, she recommends Abducting Abby, the first in her Dragon Lords of Valdier Series

Or if you prefer a Paranormal or Time Travel with a twist, you can check out <u>Lily's Cowboys</u> or <u>Indiana Wild</u>...

About S. E. Smith

S. E. Smith is a *New York Times*, *USA TODAY* and *#1 International Amazon* Bestselling author who has always been a romantic and a dreamer. An avid writer, she has spent years writing, although it has usually been technical papers for college. Now, she spends her evenings and weekends writing and her nights dreaming up new stories. An affirmed "geek," she spends her days working on computers and other peripherals. She enjoys camping and traveling when she is not out on a date with her favorite romantic guy.

Made in the USA
Lexington, KY
25 April 2015